MW01253798

THINGS I CAN'T CHANGE

by

T.F. Pruden

Copyright © 2022 by T.F. Pruden

T.F. PRUDEN

Other books by T.F. Pruden

A Dog and His Boy
Grand Opening
One Fate Befalls
The Recalcitrant P.I.
Where Some Roads End
Refugees of Confederation

1st Edition

Published 2023
by
Solitary Press
a division of
1986041 Alberta Ltd.

Cover

T-BIRD
by
Lonigan Gilbert

T.F. PRUDEN

For my brother Blair and our good friend Stu.

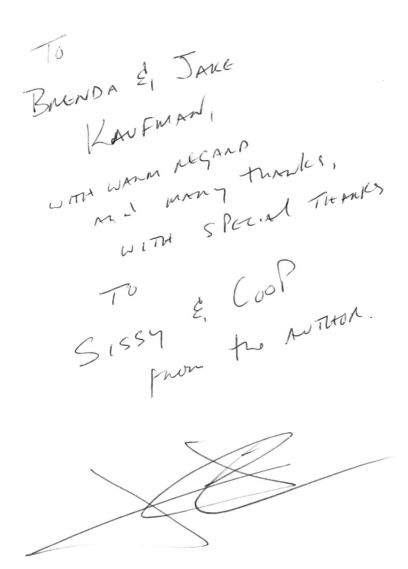

T.F. PRUDEN

CONTENTS

T.F. PRUDEN

ONE

"I have no proof for this," I said, "but since giving the stuff up, it seems clear enough, to me, anyway, that I was born an alcoholic."

I read from a printed sheet, heavily wrinkled, spread open on the dais in front of me. Before speaking again, I paused and looked up, towards a silent, but unseen, and waiting crowd. I could not see them because of the glare from the stage lights pointed at me.

As I took a breath, the black letters on the white page swam for a near imperceptible second, then gathered themselves, turning back into words as I exhaled.

We met in one of many local venues owned by a small Saskatchewan city and rented for the purpose. In the large room sat a hundred or more kindred spirits. The gathering, called a roundup by vets of the outfit, took over many of the city's public venues on the same weekend each year.

A moment earlier, my standard greeting, as Travis P., was welcomed by a warm hello from the unseen room.

I was an invited guest, and there to share my story with strangers. Just then, sweating despite the air-conditioned comfort of the space, the mic-stand doubled as a lifeline. In one hand, I had a death-grip on the gooseneck connecting it to the dais. While the other kept the sheaf of papers in place on top of it.

Beads of warmth now gathered, trapped by wisps of dark hair on the small of my back, as I smiled with melting confidence to the darkness facing me. Despite apparent middle-age and a crisp suit, for an instant, I was again the too-young boy, trying to impress, blackout drunk on his first try. A heartbeat or two later, I grinned.

"Because the first time I took a drink of booze, it led to a blackout drunk."

At the recalled picture of my younger self, I laughed out loud. From the unlit crowd, a murmur of shared laughter rippled back to me. I felt a bridge appear between us.

"I was thirteen, and having a party with a bunch of friends, and one of them, though I forget which of us it was now, must have known someone old enough to buy the booze."

The wide spot next to the lonely highway we called our home town had two liquor stores, a hotel with a vendor's license for off-sales, and a legion. There were also a couple of local bootleggers, open all night and Sundays, a remnant of another time.

Booze was plentiful if you were of legal age. Or knew someone old enough, and willing to buy it for you.

"I didn't tell anyone it was my first time, either, and gulped that firewater down like a veteran, though I nearly puked from the taste of it."

In reply, another murmur of shared knowledge rose from the unseen room. I smiled, again nodding to the darkness before continuing my story.

"Not only that, but as long as I drank, it was the same every time. There never was, not even once, a day or night when the taste of that stuff appealed to me."

Maybe here, I imagined a mild rumble.

"But only drinking more of it relieved my pain."

This time, I imagined, as they passed unseen, silent nods, repeated by many in the crowd.

"So, by the time I got to Calgary, I was twenty-three, and had been drinking, far too much, and pretty steady, since that first time. And, like many of you here, I'm sure, I didn't then think I had a problem with booze."

I paused a beat before again speaking.

"In fact, I was known as one hell of a drinker!"

From the room, the comfort of warm laughter arose. I let

go of the gooseneck and smiled again, this time giving a nod to my audience. They were more like a group of old friends than strangers I'd never met.

"I also think I've led a charmed life. Otherwise, there's no way I'd be standing here, sober for years, talking to you now."

I paused once more, recalling the young man who once wore my shoes.

"Anyway, in the years between my first blackout and throwing that fight in Calgary, I lived mostly as an occasional pro boxer, a sometime criminal, and a close-to-full-time drunk."

Those who knew me then, for many good reasons, remain surprised I survived those times.

From the darkness in front of me came a rumble of understanding. Their embrace emboldened me and I warmed to my tale. A moment later, mostly by habit, but also from need, I checked my ego.

"Because, though I was a lousy drunk and a small-time hood, I also had an aversion to work to go along with the inflated opinion of myself."

I was there for them, not me. So long as I kept it that way, I could stay sober. The minute things changed; I was the nearest drink away from drunk. Reminded, I nodded to myself before getting back to my tale.

"But I didn't come here to talk about drinking today. So, beyond a few lowlights from those times, I'm going to share the story of my recovery with you."

An audible murmur of encouragement rose from the unseen crowd.

"Like some, I'm the product of a broken home."

By then, recovery had long-ago let me either forgive or forget the worst of my family's troubles. While many of the rest have proved a source for laughs.

"Trouble with booze ran throughout the extended family, too, but when I was a kid, few of us seemed aware of it, and even less worried."

As a child, I thought everyone must drink. To the people

around me, it looked normal.

"Later, there was jail. Not serious time, but plenty of short bits. No prison. Too many drunk tanks, a fortune in fines, and don't get me started on the price of lawyers."

I paused, grinning into the waiting darkness.

"To pay for what soon became my teenage drinking habit, I dropped out of high school before graduating to take a job in the trades. By then, I liked drinking a whole lot more than school, and besides that, was pretty sure I had the whole life-deal figured out, too."

A smatter of laughter followed, and I replied with another nod and my best copy of a relaxed grin.

"Anyway, it wasn't too long before I figured out my drinking didn't suit life as a working man. Not only that, but amateur boxing didn't pay. So, when money got scarce enough, I took a pro fight."

I can't tell lies, though I'm sure the memories might sting less if I did.

"See, boxing was a romantic dream from my boyhood, but I didn't have a clue. I had a few amateur fights, and won a medal or two, in some out of the way places. And like most things that look glamorous from the outside, I soon found out it took hard work, and a dedication unknown to me, to make it in one of the world's most dangerous rackets."

There are plenty of those times I'd sooner forget.

"But, like any practicing alcoholic with a serious case of self-will running riot, I didn't let that stop me."

I grinned, recalling my chronic shortage of either fear, or common sense, in those days.

"So, because I was pale-skinned and willing, rather than overly talented, hanging around a boxing gym meant I got plenty of chances. And for a while, it looked like the party would never end. But you know how that goes, friends."

I stared a moment into the dark of wasted memory. In front of me, it reflected from the waiting pages. And, though far from opaque, the surreal blur of yesterday's oblique happenstance isn't welcomed here. In fact, and usually, it's avoided.

"Until that last dry drunk, by my late teens I had made a habit of drinking most every day."

In silence broken only by their unseen nods, I felt, more than knew, the strangers listening were my people.

"So, when I turned up, cold sober, for weigh-ins held at the old Center Inn, in downtown Calgary, I was fighting under my own name, which was a rare turn by then. And though I had stayed white-knuckle sober through a two-month training camp, I also agreed to take an early dive against a rising local prospect later that night."

With a snort of disgust, I recalled my want for a drink on that long ago evening. A palpable thing. Though my hands were steady, it had consumed my mind.

"Most times, in those days, I used a few different names to qualify for a license to fight on small-time cards held at cities throughout the Midwest."

Along with a regular crew of usual suspects, we swapped names and tried not to hurt each other while putting on a good-enough show.

I paused, reaching for the glass of water on a lower shelf of the polished wood dais. After taking a drink, I cleared my throat. Without looking at the notes in front of me, I returned to my story.

"I've been sober for quite a while, friends, but it's still tough facing who I was back then."

Though I forgave myself a long time ago, it's not a good look. I nodded in reply to the murmur of understanding rising from an unseen room filled with strangers.

"Thanks to each and every one of you. For sharing your experience, strength, and hope with me. Because if you hadn't, it's either punch drunk or dead, for this alcoholic. But instead, I'm here with you tonight, as a sober drunk I know might say, laughing and scratching."

I smiled and raised a hand, grateful for the applause but wanting to limit it. There was a schedule in place for speakers that I meant to respect.

"So, two weeks after taking that dive, I arrived, half-drunk, at Edmonton, Alberta, on a Greyhound bus."

I was near flat broke, with few prospects, and fewer friends. By then, I had betrayed everyone, and everything, that once surrounded my drunkard's life like flowers growing on a pile of horse manure.

I paused, and the memory of my last furtive drink, stolen from a mickey, emptied on the trip between the Alberta prairie cities and left on that bus, joined me onstage. I grinned, again pleased to know it was the last I had yet taken.

"My older brother was there to greet me when I stepped off that bus. And I swear, at the time, I didn't know I had already taken my last drink. In fact, though I knew he was by then a few years sober, I think my plan was to shack up with him for one night before heading out to find a drink first-thing the next day."

I paused long enough to shake my head before continuing.

"And nowadays, I accept life as whatever happens when I make other plans. Because I had no idea, the first words I spoke to my brother that night would change my life."

I know they came from somewhere inside me, and I remember saying them, but I recall no earlier intent to say any such thing. To him or anyone else.

I paused. For a moment, I was back there, watching the scene play out.

"Because, for a minute there, anyway, it was like I was under someone else's control, or at least, like there was someone else driving. That's as close as I can get to describing what it was like for me."

In my mind, I relived the moment as I shared it.

"Because, when I got off that bus, my first word to him wasn't hello."

I nodded, more to myself than to the unseen people seated in the darkened room before me.

"No, the first word out of my mouth was please. And I think I'll always remember saying this to my brother, too. Because I was close to tears when I asked him, please, can you help me learn how to live?"

I thought a sigh, disembodied but audible, though maybe only to me, rose from the pregnant dark of that unlit room. While on the stage, for just a moment, I recalled old friend Steve B., another fellow I believe much at fault for what became my lifetime of unbroken sobriety.

*

"I started practicing young," I said, "because in my family they taught you to get after it, and early, too, eh? Yup, a clan of go-getters, that's us!"

There was a large crowd assembled before me. I stood behind what looked to be a polished wood pulpit, a mobile rig, on casters, with a microphone attached to it. We gathered in a hall rented from the Saskatchewan city hosting the annual group event.

For maybe a second, I wondered if the contraption's wheels were locked.

Because I'm six feet and a couple inches in bare feet, and the lectern looked better suited to someone six inches shorter. I was leaning on it, and didn't want the thing rolling out from beneath me.

In the front row, seated on folding chairs, were my mom and dad. Only a moment before, my standard greeting, as Steve B., was welcomed by the full house.

"So, this is what I think. That I was already a practicing alcoholic by the time I got to high school. Because I was partying it up with the boys on most weekends, and heavy too, by then, you know? It also seemed like booze was easy to get in those days. And I thought I knew what normal drinking was all about, too, eh? Like, I figured everybody worked hard through the week, then went out and got whaled on weekends, like that. It sure looked like a local habit, anyway, you know?"

I paused as laughter spread from my family in the front row to the people now overfilling the room.

"Ya, I grew up thinking the 'weekend bender' was all good. So long as you kept it between the lines through the week, worked hard, and took care of business, it seemed ok to hoist a few jars to unwind after work or, in my case, school."

I smiled at the memory of my teenaged self, looking forward to the party afterwards more than graduating.

"And I had my first blackout drunk after our high school's grad, with things only getting worse from there, you know?"

I replied to the many nods in the crowd with one of my own.

"So, before I crossed the finish line, there were adventures, if you know what I mean."

I paused, gazed out to the room, and raised both eyebrows, while also shaking my head as I looked skyward. The warmth of knowing laughter, shared by what seemed everyone in the room, embraced me.

I paused a moment, loosening my tie with one hand, while raising the mic with the other, before getting on with my story.

"But don't get the wrong idea, because this ain't gonna be no drunkalogue here, and that's for sure, eh?"

I paused again, bowing my head while raising my hands to make a steeple in front of me, before getting on with it.

"I grew up in old Montreal, you know, and was what you might call one of them Anglaise speaking, life-of-the-party kind of almost-French guys, and I always knew where the best one's were in my younger day, too, eh? Comment Ca Va? With the crosscut saw, Mon Ami? Same thing goes for the Cheris, you know? Like I said, it was the times, and I enjoyed sharing a laugh."

Right there, favorite pictures from my high school yearbook passed through my rapidly aging mind.

"I was no athlete, but cutting it up at my own expense made me popular since long before I started grade school. And I loved the attention, too, eh? You bet; I did!"

By the time I got to high school, my antics were semi-legendary among a group of neighborhood friends.

"But my mom and dad believed in hard work, and so, I held part-time jobs since taking my first one delivering the local newspaper. And early saving, enforced by my parents, meant I could buy my own car when I was old enough to get a license, which helped make me even more popular, eh? There were some golden days, my friends."

I smiled at my parents, both many years sober and seated in the front row. They each returned it with one of their own, and to me at least, glowed.

A moment later, nearly overcome with gratitude, I reminded myself why I was there.

"I got into cars early, too, as a kid, eh? And while my dad encouraged my hobby, it sure wasn't his idea to make it my career."

In my teens, having a car made it easier to meet girls.

"Anyway, I guess you'd say I was a popular kid in school, too. A solid 'C' student all the way through, eh? No standout grades here, just middle of the pack, solid-citizen stuff, and dreams to match, my friends. Like I told you, I enjoyed sharing a laugh. And besides, I had an older sister who was already suffering her share of misery because of the over-achieving, you know? None of that for me, thank you, boys. I mean, that's what I'd have said, if anyone had ever asked me about it."

I paused a moment, reaching for the glass of water on the small table next to the microphone's stand. A long sip of it cooled my throat. While in my head, I recalled those teen years of increasingly heavy drinking.

Throughout those times, I kept it to the weekends. Because that's how I thought a normal person should drink.

From the seat next to my mom, my sister smiled up at me. It was like she could read my mind. The sight of her calmed me. I nodded to her before speaking to the crowd.

"I didn't miss a day of work until years later, by the way. But let me tell you, there were many shifts worked while suffering through some painful hangovers in my high school days, you know? Because, like I told you, me and the lads got after it pretty hard on the weekends, eh? Good times, we told each other!"

I stopped a moment, shaking my head at the old memory,

and grinned, before continuing my story.

"A few of my friends later went to college, but most of us went straight to work out of high school. It seems funny nowadays, but back then, all the way, since grade school, you were told to think about spending a lifetime working at one thing. You wanted to find that thing while you were young, too, so you could do it until you were old. Your career, whatever it was, would be spent doing that one thing, hopefully for the same company, until you retired with a pension in some far away, but reliable future, right?"

A murmur, of what I presumed awareness, rippled through the crowd in front of me. By now, most of us have learned the story was a fantasy told by rich people, meant to keep poor ones from cracking under the strain of bitter reality.

"At the time, I wasn't interested in much beyond cars and girls, you know? So, maybe that's why the car business looked like a natural career choice, for me, after grad."

In high school, I took a job working for a car dealer, prepping new cars for delivery.

"And what I remember most about those early days, really my biggest memory, is that no matter how many people were around, and no matter whether I was drunk or sober, I always felt, every time, alone in the crowd, you know?"

It was a lingering discomfort, like a bellyache that never went away.

"Even when every pair of eyes in a room were on me, I somehow never felt a part of anything, eh? Like, at the same time, I craved something, but I couldn't tell you what it might be, not exactly, anyway, and that's for sure."

I nodded in silent reply to many from my audience. The world's troubles didn't put a drink in my hand. That was me. But even then, I remember seeing how the standard narrative could never work for many of us.

"And by the time I started high school, in my stomach, an uneasy feeling, about everything, seemed to have made itself a home."

Despite a growing discomfort, I said nothing to anyone.

"So, for me, drinking was kind of like filling a hole in my gut, that never seemed to get enough of whatever it was I wanted, you know? And I had no idea what that was, eh? I mean, I guess I thought it was normal. So, I didn't ever say anything to anybody about it, either, you know? But, by the time I got to high school, I knew one thing for sure."

I looked again at my parents. In their eyes, I found strength.

"Booze made me feel better, no matter what kind of pain life gave me."

As I spoke, I raised my gaze to the room. From among the unseen crowd rose another murmur of shared awareness. I nodded to the darkness and smiled, grateful to be there.

"Every time I drank, all through my high school days, I felt better after a few than I did beforehand, you know? Not that I wasn't well enough set, either, eh? It was a fine home where I was raised, where both mom and dad worked hard. And despite Pop having his own tough times with the bottle, they held it together until getting it together, you know? They didn't expose us kids to many of their nightmares, and we're grateful for that, too, eh? We had it pretty good, and I knew it, even then. And hey, love you guys, you know?"

I nodded to my parents as applause rose from the room. But when I looked up a moment later, it soon quieted.

"Because there's worse things than middle-class and suburban, and that's what I aspired to, eh? What my folks had earned for themselves seemed about right, for me, too, anyway, you know? And maybe everyone felt alone and separated from everybody and everything else in the world, the way I did when I was a kid. That's what I thought, eh? I mean, everyone I knew drank, or at least, that's what I figured. And I also believed everybody, aside from maybe a few of the religious types, must use and enjoy the stuff, at least as much as I did, for the same reason, you know?"

I can't say why, but right there, the memory of Blaine T., who is likely the best friend I ever had, either drunk or sober, popped into my head. Maybe it's because, most of the time, I blame him for both getting and keeping me sober.

*

"Anyhow, I was barely fifteen when a Winnipeg judge told me six months in juvenile detention would set me straight," I said, "and friends, you gotta know I meant to prove that ess-oh-bee wrong."

I smiled at the laughter in response to my quip. Only a moment earlier, the room replied to the outfit's standard greeting from Blaine T., with the warmth of a shared hello.

In front of me, every seat in the northern Saskatchewan city's convention center hall looked to be filled. My hand shook as I reached for the tall glass of water waiting on a fitted cloth-covered table next to the dais where I stood.

With a dry throat lubed, I went on with my story.

"Because I was an angry young man and had been since my father passed away only a couple of years before that. I was also an Indigenous kid in a white man's world and hated myself for it."

I paused, again recalling the long-ago day we lost my dad. When the ache passed, I returned to sharing.

"My mom had four kids with my dad before he passed, and four more with the good man who later did his best to be our stepfather. They worked hard to make a home for us, and I know all of them did everything they could to make our lives as safe and comfortable as possible, under the hardest of circumstances."

I felt, more than heard, what might have been a wave, of what I guessed was something like compassion, pass through the listening crowd.

"I was my dad's oldest son, and always felt a strong duty to look out for my younger siblings, too. There were only a couple of years between each of us, and I was tightest with the brother closest to me in age."

My brother Val was my best friend.

"From birth, we were each other's best friend, and I'm sorry to say he followed me into a life of crime. Of course, as I could later say the same thing about the others, too, that wasn't what made him special."

I paused, waiting out another wave of recalled pain before again speaking.

"Because our parents would each have their troubles with booze, that soon enough tore them, and our home, apart. We kids were the collateral damage."

Drugs took my brother at twenty-three.

"And I'm no scientist, but it sure looks like genetics might have something to say about our shared illness. It seemed to touch all of us, in some form, anyhow."

In our family, they bought booze in bulk.

"But, just like when my dad passed away ten years earlier, when my brother died at twenty-three from a drug overdose, the only thing that relieved the pain, for me, was booze."

Maybe before that, I was looking for something but had yet to find it.

"And I think it started taking over, with me, from about then, but who can say for sure? I might have been sick with it since birth, for all I know, but it didn't really show up until after my dad was gone, I guess."

I reached for the glass, and reminded myself to keep things straight, before taking a cooling sip. Along with the water, a sense of calm flowed into me. I held the glass in my hand when I next spoke.

"By the way, everyone in the family lost their status as government-approved Indians when our mom remarried, too, but I was mad at the world long before then. And though I blamed him for plenty at the time, our stepdad, a Metis man but also without a government stamp of approval, had little to do with either the anger or my drinking. I know that now and have nobody but you folks to thank for it."

I nodded to the room, then took another sip from the water glass. Sharing the hard words was a tonic. After saying them, courage took root in my belly. I cleared my throat before again speaking.

"By then, we were already living off the reservation, anyhow. And for quite a while, too. We were poor folks, sure, but my dad worked construction in Winnipeg, and my mom kept house for rich strangers living in another part of town, while we four kids went to school."

To me, those times are remembered as the happiest days of my childhood.

"It was a good life, friends, despite lots of what was, in those days, normal racism and bigotry. Because back then, in this country, if you were born into a visible minority group, they put you into a lower class within society."

I paused, recalling countless taunts exchanged with different colored kids sharing the neighborhood through my childhood years.

"It was automatic and came with the territory."

At the time, public demonstrations of bigotry and racism were also routine.

"But there was no awareness of what it might be like for people living otherwise when I was a kid."

Sadly, back then, it was the only world anyone living where we did had ever known.

"So, you grew up feeling the hatred everyone has for you, and your kind, because it's in the air, and surrounds you, everywhere, all the time. And you learn quick there's no getting away from it, no matter where you might go, either."

I nodded to a low rumble passing through the crowd in response to my statement.

"Maybe it shames you, but as a kid, you're only aware of the pain filling your insides whenever you run into it."

In those days, that meant daily.

"I know that kind of anger turns into hatred quick enough though, when every day you hear your mom and dad called a 'dirty Indian', and much worse, by shopkeepers, school teachers, neighbors, and friends."

Another murmur, this one louder, came from the dark in

reply. I raised a hand, thanking the strangers for their assumed support.

"After my dad passed, all of that stuff started to bother me a lot more than it ever had when he was here, too."

Once again, I was grateful that for me, the flames of youthful anger had been tempered by the waters of mature acceptance. Nowadays, I try to spend more time dealing with my own failings, and less on those of my fellow's.

"Anyhow, by the time I went into what they called youth detention the first time, I was a couple of years into my career as a hard case. On the outside, by then I ran the games played by a loose-knit group of teens that put me in there."

I didn't plan on taking any crap from anyone I met in there, either.

"Not only that, but within a week of landing in that joint, I had gone through enough of the so-called tough guys to earn a spot at the first table."

I paused again, but ignored the water, and the lingering fear, now jumping in my belly, raised by the specter of my younger self.

"Here's how it went. On my first day there, a friend from back home, in for a few months already before I got there, pointed out a big white boy, who claimed to be among the toughs running the joint."

The young fellow looked a little too full of himself, to me, with curly blonde hair and what looked to be too-many teeth for him to shut his mouth.

"So, after dinner, I followed him to his barracks, and put the boots to him where everyone could watch me do it. From then on, for as long as I was there, whenever I could, I tormented him, too."

I shook my head at the remembered cruelty. And reminded myself again how racism is rooted in ignorance.

"By then, it was my standard move, and would be, so long as I made my living on the streets. Find out who was supposed to be toughest and get after him. No quarter. Either asked or given.

But that first time inside barely introduced what was coming for me."

I nodded to the darkness again before speaking. And reminded myself how strongly like attracts its own kind.

"Because I didn't really start drinking seriously until after I got out of detention that first time. Even after my dad died, though I went on a heavy bender, it didn't last long."

Before going inside, I partied now and then, but learning the small-time crime trade meant I needed to keep a cool head.

"That's why, in the early days, I was mostly sober when committing the theft and property crimes that made my money."

The nod I gave was meant for me, but my confession raised a knowing rumble from the crowd in reply.

"And so, long before my brothers later followed suit, I dropped out of school when my mom split up with my stepdad. Like I told you before, I blamed the guy for a lot, but who can say if he could have done anything to make losing our dad hurt any less that it did? Or, if doing so, might have made a difference?"

For the first time since before I introduced myself, I looked at my mom, seated in the front row, only feet from the stage on which I stood. There, she was surrounded by friends and members of our extended family. I returned her smile.

Then, I recalled her lengthy sobriety. Her struggles inspired me, and later, helped me survive my own.

"From there, until after I got sober more than fifteen years later, western Canada's jails were my most regular address."

I started with overnights in the local drunk tank.

"The stretches would get longer, and my attitude grow worse, along with my drinking, as the years went by."

In response, the rustle of a collective nod swept through the crowd in front of me.

"But I'm not here to share war stories. I'm here to talk about recovery. Oh, don't get me wrong, I know there's a time and place for that stuff, but tonight isn't it. And aside from a few of the lowlights, I'm going to share my love and gratitude for the many blessings this outfit and its people have given me, with you."

As I once again drank from the water glass, a rumble of applause filled the room.

TWO

"There's a thing that needs repeating, and right now, before I go any further."

I paused and looked out to the room before again speaking.

"I'm an alcoholic."

The room, nearly as one, nodded back in reply.

"Notice how I used the word 'am', there? And not 'was', or 'when'?"

I intended the reminder for me, not my listeners.

"I like to remind myself now and then. Because, after going such a long time without a drink, I can sometimes, almost, forget that I suffer from a progressive, and life-threatening, illness."

Once more, I paused to nod at the room.

"See, they call what I got alcoholism, not 'wasm'. And the thing is, forgetting I have it, is just another part of what makes my disease so insidious."

While I shook my head, a murmur of reply passed through the crowd. Many of them understood what I was saying.

"Not only that, but my early days of trying to get sober were nothing special, either."

When not getting jail time, I instead got sent for treatment. A few times.

"So, between trips to jail, there was treatment. Where I would dry out, and a month later, think everything was ok. A week, or sometimes two, after getting out, I would have one."

I nodded and paused, but only long enough to smile.

"Maybe as a reward, after a long day of work, but more often, to soothe my feelings if something didn't go my way. A day, or a few, later, I'd find myself back into a habit of daily drinking."

Through my middle and late twenties, it became a routine.

"After that, it wouldn't be long before I was out of work, and back to doing crime. Later, if I could avoid a trip to jail, it took being locked in a treatment center to make me stop."

As I hit my thirties, routine treatment was another habit.

"I was sick, alright."

I paused a moment, shaking my head at the memory.

"But just the same, I'm not gonna claim a healthy dose of the martyr complex wasn't a big part of my illness, because like I told you before, I had some funny ideas about duty, and family, and stuff like that, when I was a drinking man. On top of a deep shame about my heritage, it was quite a cocktail, alright."

As I cleared my throat, for a second, a wave of misplaced anger passed through me. For a moment, I felt unsteady on my feet. A second or two later, the feeling was gone.

"Maybe it was losing my dad when I was young that gave me the macho outlook on life and the world. I don't know about that, but I know being a 'man's man' was a big deal to me. As near as I can tell, from my earliest days, too. Sports and the construction trades appealed to me."

I took another sip of water, and for a moment, in my head, relived a few of the best days of my life.

"Hockey was my favorite sport when I was a kid. Baseball was second, but it was more to me than a summer pastime. I took those games seriously, the way a boy does, and loved playing them, too."

As a child, playing sports took much of my free time.

"And I enjoyed the company of 'men of the world' most of all, guys who had been around, either to war, like my dad, or in jail, like many cousins, got my respect. That was long before I ever went to jail myself, too."

My dad was my first, best, and last hero.

"But to me, after I got out of reform school the first time, the world was forever split between Rounders and Square-Johns. There was no in-between. In those days, on the streets of Winnipeg, you either knew what was going on, or had it done to you."

To me, back then, only Rounders knew the real score.

"What I wanted most, as a teen, was to be one of those men who knew the score. Not only that, but I didn't care what I had to do, or who I had to hurt, to get to be one of them, either."

I shook my head at the memory. After my dad passed, there were plenty of things I wanted to say, but there was no longer anyone to tell. At least, no one I trusted enough to talk to about that kind of stuff.

Nor could there ever be again, is what I thought then.

"Anyhow, here's a story that shows what I'm trying to say."

Before starting it, I recalled my youthful ignorance and smiled. Later, I had learned how anger often fools a man into cutting himself off from the things he most needs and truly wants. But I didn't know it then.

"I forget now, exactly why they let me out early. Or even how I found out where my baby stepbrothers were being fostered, after I hit the street. I was twenty-one and done with my first adult bit in the Headingley jail. Unknown to me, the boys were living away from their dad's remote farm so they could go to school. Beyond visiting, I don't even recall if there was a plan made to hijack them beforehand. All that's clear is, what I did then, would be called kidnapping today."

I nodded to the crowd in front of me. Their shared intake of breath was, from where I stood, loud enough for me to hear it.

"To me, once I got there, it might have seemed like I was rescuing my brothers from the clutches of 'the man' or something. I don't know. Though, I have to say, I had no clear idea of who or what 'the man' might be, then. And I will also tell you, though I bet I don't have to, that I was loaded."

To hatch the plan, I had to be. I shook my head, along with the crowd before me.

"Years later, because of taking the steps, I was forced to face my stepdad's neighbors to make amends. And I'll always be grateful to them, too. Because they chose not to have me arrested, from their own sense of decency, I guess. Such were the untold blessings granted to this practicing alcoholic, my friends."

I nodded to the room before continuing.

"And for many things in life, by now, I've learned better than to ask for rational answers. I'm just glad the man upstairs always seems to have a plan for me, no matter how often I try messing it up."

I took another sip from the water glass.

"Anyhow, after talking our way into their sleeping home, my then girlfriend and I rushed to dress the boys, or rather, I remember her struggling to get them dressed, after our getting there woke them up, along with everyone else in the house."

Even in faded memory, the moment could, easily, have become one of high drama.

"The boys were cranky, if I recall correctly, and maybe even crying, at first, but they cheered up when told we were taking them home to see their dad, I think. And in what seemed only minutes, to me, anyhow, I stole them from their foster home."

I shook my head as the faded picture passed through my mind. Once again, the nerve needed to dream up such a stunt, let alone pull it off, was more than sober me could imagine.

"I don't remember what I told the foster-parents, but knowing how I did things back then, I'm sure it would have been the biggest lie I could figure out on short notice. Like, somebody in the family being dead, or close to it. But like I told you, those kind people decided to humor me that night."

And by doing so, kept everyone safe.

"Again, for reasons of their own, they let us in, and allowed us to leave with the two boys without too much trouble."

I was not only drunk, but armed, that night. Despite the warm stage lights, a shudder passed through me. I don't enjoy recalling that stuff but can only say how it was. Because of that, I get to stay sober.

"I don't think I had any real idea, either, that I was putting my brothers in danger. At the time, drinking and driving was pretty common, if not encouraged. So, bombed at the wheel, with kids in the car, wasn't rare. Adult men, meanwhile, in many families, were believed guardians, by lots of folks in those days."

I nodded to myself at the thought of patriarchy's rule over society everywhere.

"But there's no way I can say, now, what I might have thought about it. At least, not for sure. Because I had crossed over into a blackout drunk by then."

In the context of those times, I was an elder brother. And being of legal age, was likely believed a guardian. Though I showed up, drunk, armed, and in the middle of the night. To demand an unplanned visit with my underage stepbrothers, fostering at the home of people unknown to me.

"How did the boys survive it? How did I avoid going to jail? How could logic explain such unlikely blessings?"

For those questions, I don't have any answers. None that will satisfy reason, anyhow. But I can't deny the experience.

"So, like I told you before, I'm always grateful the man upstairs has a plan, because most of the time, I sure don't."

I smiled as light applause rose from the room. Just then, with the usual good timing, pleasant thoughts of my buddy Steve B., and his search for what I call the man upstairs, crossed my mind.

*

"Not only that," I said, "but I try not to get too guilty about it. Though, since getting sober, I've done my best to be more aware of my privilege."

I looked out to the room, and, raising my eyebrows along with my shoulders, with both palms open, extended my arms. As, by now, I too am aware of the good fortune that comes with Caucasian birth.

"Besides, it ain't like this disease discriminates, eh? I mean, the bottle didn't care about the color of my skin, you know. And by the way, I doubt it took note of yours either, believe it or not."

I nodded to the murmur that rose in response to my comments.

"But I also know that plenty of folks have had it tougher than me. Though not only because of the color of my skin. Which, and there's no hiding it, is white as snow."

I nodded to a sprinkle of laughter in reply to my attempt at humor.

Then I paused for a breath. And reminded myself to get back to my story. My job wasn't preaching against the bigotry and racism ruling this world. Nor trying to relieve my guilt, for a lifetime spent giving tacit approval to it.

"And I can remember one thing, about as clear as right this minute, eh, and that's for sure, you know. But I was only fourteen the first time I heard it. Some things stick with you, I guess."

I licked my lips and wondered at how dry they were. Before speaking again, I sipped from the water glass.

"Because while I'm from a Montreal family that's a little better off than a lot of others in this outfit, I also know how lucky I was to have some good examples in my life, too, eh?"

I nodded as pictures of a comfortable red brick home, little sullied by booze-filled nightmares, rushed into my head. There, among school friends of similar means, the times went on changing, without giving much thought to us.

"Not only that, but right about then, in that Anglaise part of the city where we lived, we were forced to deal with changes happening in the province and the world beyond us, you know?"

For many of us, more than the times were changing.

"Everyone I knew seemed pretty worked up about things. Awareness of a new world order taking shape was everywhere, you know, especially among people older than me."

Not everyone agreed with the changes.

"But me, well, I was too busy chasing a party to notice much of anything in those days. I mean, even the FLQ didn't make much of a dent. Though it was dinner table talk between my parents, and many of their friends, for a while around our house."

There followed a minor exodus among the Anglaise in our neighborhood.

"It's not like my parents didn't care, either. It was because,

33

just then, in our family, there were other things needing attention."

Lucky for us, there was help nearby.

"And right there, my uncle stepped in to show me how this program worked. Though I didn't know it at the time, eh?"

Later, it meant plenty to me.

"See, my uncle was once a skid row drunk, you know, but he's now been sober for more than forty years. It was him that introduced my dad to this program."

I smiled as the face of my elderly, but patient, uncle passed through my mind's eye. No longer well enough for travel, he was not there with us.

"After my uncle got sober, he passed the message along to my dad. And though dad didn't give up the boozing right away, his brother didn't quit on him."

While my dad struggled to get it, my uncle's nightly knock at our door became a welcome routine.

"Like it does for many of us, it took Pop a few tries."

From the front row, seated next to mom, my dad's warm smile beamed at me. My uncle's support for his brother has never wavered.

"Anyway, that was the first contact I ever had with a sober drunk, and it was a big deal, you know? I mean, I loved my dad, and I didn't know what was wrong with him, but I knew it must be something bad, eh? Otherwise, why was my uncle making the nightly visits? And where did they go together? It was quite a household mystery for a while."

I nodded to the house in front of me.

"Because times were different, and neither my sister nor I had the nerve to ask anyone about it, back then, you know. And seeing my uncle, sober and living a better life, after being a bum on the street, helping my dad quit the booze, turned out to be a pretty big deal, for me."

I didn't know it, but years later, that memory helped me reach out. Maybe as much or more than anything else.

"But the thing I told you I can still remember; it was from

before my dad got sober. And I doubt I'll ever forget it."

For a second, or maybe two, I hesitated before speaking. There's no way I'll ever forget the sound.

"It was listening to his dry heaves every morning before he left for work."

The recalled sound of his pitiful suffering, which I imagined as that of a wounded animal, came at once to mind.

"I knew it was booze making him do that, and, even then, I remember hoping I would never get that way."

A tiny shudder, stirred by the distant but still painful ache of those memories, passed through me.

"Maybe it was the first time I knew what shame felt like, you know? I'm not sure. Not now, and certainly not then. But something about it scared me."

A few months after my uncle started coming around, I recall my dad's morning episodes, hidden, always, behind the closed door of the John upstairs, stopped.

"But when I started drinking, that memory haunted me a little, at first, you know? I promised myself, early on, too, that if I ever got those things because of drinking, it was time to quit."

It was among the first of many promises I'd break in pursuit of a drink.

"My dad's get-togethers with his brother carried on, all through the rest of the years I lived with my folks. Eventually, like I told you before, my dad stopped drinking."

By the time they moved away, he'd been sober for a few years.

"And despite my early promise, I suffered countless cases of dry heaves, later, on my journey as a practicing alcoholic."

I smiled, as a murmur of what I hoped was understanding rose from the people seated in front of me. A moment later, I went on with the preamble to my story.

"And did I say that my older sister has also been sober three years longer than me?"

I smiled at her, and from the seat next to our mom, she grinned back at me. I waited for a ripple of applause to pass before speaking.

"So, as you can see, it's really been a family affair for us. And nowadays, I'm most grateful the man upstairs made sure I had some real good examples to look at along the way, right there at home."

I grinned at my family in the front row.

"Not only that, but right from my very first meeting, he made sure I ran into a bunch more, too, you know."

Just then, the memory of my good buddy Travis P., another sober drunk I won't soon forget, horned in on me. He's my sponsor's younger brother, and the three of us once shared a house together, as bachelor roommates, in the west end of Edmonton, Alberta. Near at once, a smile creased my face. As usual, when thinking of Travis, it was genuine.

*

"And I sure didn't think," I said, "that learning how to live would mean giving up the booze!"

I paused again and grinned at the darkness facing me.

"Because by then, it was among the last of my friends."

I waited a moment as a ripple of laughter passed through the room.

"Of course, that should've been no surprise, given my routine crazy. Here's how things went in my teenage years."

My first birthday drunk, and its resulting blackout, soon became something of a personal tradition.

"Not long after getting over that first brutal hangover, which, of course, closely followed blackout drunk number one, the birthday of a now-forgotten school buddy led to a similar escapade."

That first hangover was, sadly, no worse than the many shameful acts committed while drunk before it. The second one proved no better.

"Based on those first couple of tries, my local rep was made, and soon enough, drinking parties in the bush got to be a habit, with me as the de facto ringleader, among a group of teen friends and distant relatives."

Though starting early, a long time passed before I heard

anyone say a word against my drinking.

"And, because our parties happened on weekends, and away from home, in the company of friends, there was little said about my drinking. My bachelor dad, who by then had separated from our mom, was a farmer and worked hard, every day, from sunup until dark, scraping a living out of that place. He had no time for babysitting teenage boys."

By the time I ran off to the city, my underage drinking was routine.

"I don't recall much being said about my age, either."

I reached for the water glass and took a sip. As my throat cooled, near at once, a faded memory bloomed. I smiled, and looking away from my prepared notes, unsure, but feeling a momentary insight, decided to share it.

The remembrance of a birthday more than twenty years past unfolded before me. Though revealing, it won't ever be one of my prouder moments.

"After running away to live in the city early in my teens, I built a rep for celebrating big dates, like holidays, or long weekends, but also, and especially, birthdays. Not only my own, but those of friends. I figured any of them were worth a blowout."

I did my best to take advantage of the opportunities, too.

"Of course, by the time my eighteenth birthday came around, I was primed for a big deal, and wanted the party to be legendary."

I sipped again from the water glass, and smiled as I recalled the sick boy, trying to become a man, despite it.

"By then, I had already dropped out of school, after moving into the city, to go looking for work."

That statement is not, entirely, a lie. But it isn't wholly true, either.

"At fifteen, I had run away from my dad's country life, to search for one of my own, in the big city of Winnipeg. And plainly, he knew his son well enough. Because he didn't bother asking me to come home."

Back then, I didn't know what I wanted. But I was sure it wasn't to be found on that lonely Manitoba farm.

"For a year or two, I lived as a street kid, and enjoyed it, too. But I had friends and relatives working at all kinds of things in town, and it wasn't tough finding my way. So, by the time that eighteenth birthday came around, I had a good-sized network and a rep of my own to go along with it."

Even then, I knew better than to think anyone envied it.

"Anyway, small-time crime was already a big part of my scene in those days, and I was getting known, in some places, for peddling a little dope, and in others, for not being shy about mixing it up on the sidewalk."

In those days, I loved to fight, either on the street or in a boxing ring.

"Up to that point, an unknown and still green amateur boxer, I was keeping my boozing habit mostly under control."

Even then, it was a struggle.

"And despite my all-too-common freedom thirty-five dreams, I was little more than a dime-bag dealing punk in those days."

My ego was surely bigger than my accomplishments.

"There was back then a small hotel on Albert Street, in downtown Winnipeg, with a patio restaurant under a clear glass canopy facing the street. The older sister of a friend of mine waitressed in the place. In those days, she was quite a looker, but also picky, with no taste for underage toughs like me. And I, of course, carried a torch for her."

I nodded, while a grin played across my lips at the memory of her many refusals.

"Now, it's worth knowing that Canada lowered the legal drinking age to eighteen the same year I reached it. And let me tell you, I was sure pleased by that."

By then, I had taken up the drink to get drunk, not to have fun, creed.

"So, on my eighteenth birthday, in that restaurant, in the company of my good friend, her younger brother, and quite loaded, I made the waitress another pitch. Which she, as usual, shot down, in explicit detail."

I paused a moment, and felt the memory pass over me, before taking a sip of water to soothe my scarred teenage pride.

"And when she was done with me, there I sat, an angry young wannabe rounder, just turned eighteen, who believed himself heartbroken, after a lengthy afternoon of heavy drinking."

I hardly remember the scene, as by then I was loaded.

"Nowadays, I can barely recall sitting at the restaurant's table, let alone the rest of what happened. But I was drunk enough to slur, I was later told. And more shamed, I'm sure, by her public refusal, than hurt by it."

To friends there with me, the scene could scarcely have been funnier.

"When a birthday cake showed up, it must have been too late to do me any good. I don't even know who cut it, or who was partying with me there, by then. As I have no pictures from the event, I suppose I never will."

Given what later happened, it's likely better for my ego.

"Because much of that day is only a blur now. So, I don't dispute what anyone might say about what took place. Nor did I try back then. The charges were all true, and there was no doubt about my guilt, either. And though I would later claim drinking too much was at fault, there was no hiding from what I did."

I heard, but could not see, movement, as many people shifted in unison, uncomfortable in their seats. And I believed they knew my need was not to confess, but to share a lived insight, and kept speaking.

"Later, booze would often make an ass out of me, but this was the first time it led directly to a crime."

Only then did I pause. And, maybe, imagined a collective intake of breath.

"Did I mention being a regular customer of the restaurant? Or that it was, once upon a time ago, a well-known watering hole for many of Winnipeg's rounders? Well, those are the unfortunate facts. Not only that, but as an underage wannabe on the way up in the trade, everyone who worked at the place knew me."

Fortunately, there are things I can't forget.

"The birthday party was no secret, either, and me and three of my then-pals got started early, with drinks in the bar before lunch."

In those days, I wasn't alone in believing birthday's a big deal among my crew.

"Our tab followed us into the restaurant for cocktails with a light lunch, and back into the bar for an afternoon of draft beers while shooting pool."

The party started at opening time, which was an hour before noon in those days.

"With an early steak dinner, enjoyed by a larger crowd of friends, along with many shots of premium liquor, followed by the afore-mentioned birthday cake, later added to it."

Because I was a well-known young player, through the lengthy afternoon, my fast-growing tab raised little concern.

"I have no defense for what came later and having to admit what I did shames me to this day."

I paused again, and looked out at the room, wearing what I knew was a rueful grin.

"Because, drunk or sober, some things are beneath contempt."

Though a long time has since passed, I still believe that.

"And so, you can imagine how it felt the next day, when friends told me I had pulled a dine-and-dash on the restaurant and bar tab for my birthday party!"

For a moment, with what was, to me, the sound of collective relief, a wave of laughter filled the room. In reply, I could only smile and shake my head. Even years later, it's the only fall from grace that continues to embarrass me.

As once again, much as it had then, my drinking made me the butt of a joke.

THREE

"It was a little more than a year later, when, by accident, I took the 'Twenty Questions' test the first time."

I grinned as the memory of a long-ago day crossed my mind.

"But I doubt you can imagine how proud I was to do so well on that test."

I paused as laughter spread in reply to the comment.

"I didn't even study for it, but made only two mistakes!"

This time, chuckling along with the room stopped me. A moment later, still wearing a smile, I went on with my story.

"I'm pretty sure that many of us have either seen or been asked the twenty questions on that simple test. In fact, I'm going to say a lot of us here tonight have taken it, and maybe even a few times."

To me, it was a murmur of approval that rose from the room in reply.

"But when my big brother shared a copy with me, it was the first time I'd ever seen the damned thing."

I smiled again at the still-fresh memory.

"By then, our mom had already told me he was no longer drinking. As he lived in Calgary in those days, I didn't give it too much thought. But when he came home on holiday that summer, and we hung out, he didn't touch the booze."

He wanted nothing to do with it. For me, things were off, as if a barrier stood between us.

"Only a couple of years before, he was my favorite drinking buddy. But, just like that, it was like we had nothing in common."

At least, that's how it was, though only for a while, to me.

"But he didn't try selling me anything, and so, his not drinking turned out not to be much of a thing, after all. He was still my bud, and we've been close for as long as I can remember, despite the fifteen years between us."

To this writing, my brother Blaine remains among my closest friends.

"Anyway, it was soon plain that we'd be talking about some different stuff, now that he didn't drink, than we used to when he did."

I paused for another sip from the water glass.

"But let me tell you, there were other differences that showed up. Even though there was little sign of physical changes, he sure drank a lot of coffee. And I guessed that was what gave him so much energy. Anyway, to me, then, I recall thinking that my newly sober brother might turn out to be quite a pain in the ass."

I nodded, smiling at the memory.

"Pardon my language. One thing we didn't ever talk about, though, was my drinking."

I remember, right away, and for reasons unknown, how that surprised me. I was, maybe, a little disappointed.

"Nor did he say anything to me about going to meetings, or getting sober, or any kind of stuff like that."

Instead, he was my brother. Not the same, but not much different. He no longer touched booze. That part was, for me, unnerving.

"We hung out, just like old times, except without the drinking we had always shared, and, I thought, enjoyed."

I remember the sameness of his personality, in those early days of his return, threw me.

"So, instead of boozing, we talked. About plenty of things we did before, and even some stuff we never had. And, after a little while, anyway, it was no longer strange. Because he was ok, and a lot like his old self. It wasn't long before we fell into talking about all kinds of family and personal stuff. Like we always did, before he went off and gave up the booze."

I paused for another sip from the water glass before continuing.

"He never brought up booze, either, or anything to do with

my drinking, as I recall. But somehow, he let me know that not drinking was improving his life. At least, that's what I got from a lot of our talks."

I looked out to the room then and grinned before again speaking.

"It was also clear, in the form of a new car, nice clothes, ample cash, and credit cards, that his life was better than it had been when he was drinking. And more than anything he said, that impressed me."

There was no denying the signs of material success. To me, a young rounder trying to make his way on the street, in those days, nothing spoke louder.

"Somehow, and plainly, something about my big brother had changed. He was no longer the gangster he lived as when I knew him a few years earlier. He had transformed into some unknown white-collar working dude, and looked to be making plenty of money doing it, too. I didn't know how not drinking made any difference to all that, but I was sure enticed by his shiny new lifestyle."

I nodded, warmed by the memory.

"Throughout a three-week holiday spent among our family at Winnipeg that summer, he mainly told stories about fun and games, enjoyed with new friends, at his Alberta home."

While he didn't say so, it was plain that his friends, out there, in the great unknown, did not drink.

"And no matter how closely I looked, at no time did I see him change, or in any way, revert to his former self."

He had neither fear nor interest in booze. Not only that, but crime was no longer part of his life.

"The other big thing, aside from the not drinking, for me, that changed with him, was that he no longer did crime. None. Never, according to him."

To me, it was uncanny.

"But, aside from that, he was cool, and seemed like his normal old self in some ways, but also, in ways that I couldn't really figure out, he was quite a bit different."

For unknown reasons, not drinking made him more interesting, too, not less. And that surprised me, maybe as much as anything else.

"It seemed like he knew stuff, about the world, and himself, and me, too."

I paused, recalling those early days and my first look at our sober brother. In our family, he looked, to ignorant me, to be a unicorn.

"At the time, I recall thinking that it was, almost, like not drinking booze had made him smarter."

I nodded, more to myself than the room, at the memory. Even back then, when confronted by it up close, I had a hard time denying reality.

"But like I told you, he didn't say a word to me about boozing, and even bought my drinks whenever we were out for meals. Which happened on most days he was around that summer, by the way. And at no time did I feel like he was checking me out, either. He was my big brother, and except for not drinking, he was the same guy I thought I always knew, or maybe even a better version of himself."

I paused a moment, thinking of those days.

"So, along with many others in the extended family, I was shocked when he took no interest in drinking that summer."

Blaine was content, and not even concerned by other people drinking around him.

"To me, though nobody said anything, it maybe seemed like more than a few people, including myself, were disappointed when he didn't return to drinking with us."

I remember keeping that idea to myself, too, then.

"But eventually, curiosity got the better of me, and so, maybe a week before he returned to Alberta, I asked him who he was going to see, alone, for a couple of hours each day."

By then, playing the role of watchful secret agent full time, I had noticed him going off on his own for a while, sometimes in the afternoon, other times in the evening. Over the weeks of his visit home, it happened daily, and became a routine.

"Because after hanging around him for a couple of weeks, I was just about certain there must be a woman he was meeting somewhere when he was gone every day, like that."

I didn't know there were regular program group meetings happening through many hours of the day or night, across the city.

"So, that's when my big brother first told me about the program meetings. And he didn't try to hide anything about them, either. They were his medicine, he told me, then. For people like him, he claimed, the meetings worked something like insulin did for diabetics. But he didn't preach, or suggest I go to one with him."

I remember being relieved when he didn't.

"But what he told me was surprising, too."

At the time, I recall playing it cool, and doing my best not to show it.

"I tried not to let on and said nothing to him about that. But from then on, whenever he would leave for what I figured was one of those meetings, I gave him a nod. And didn't again ask him about the business."

I recollect being relieved when he didn't push it.

"Maybe it made me uncomfortable thinking about him as a sick person? I don't know. But something made me leave it alone."

Even now, I'm not sure what it was.

"Because I wanted my brother to be okay. But I didn't want to talk about what was keeping him that way. Or what had caused him to be unwell in the first place. And one day, maybe a weekend later, and only a day or two before he left for Alberta, I found a copy of the twenty questions in his car."

A rectangle of yellow paper fell out of the glove box when I dug around looking for a pack of gum, and on it was printed the test.

"It was after we had lunch in a downtown restaurant together. As usual that summer, I was eating on his dime. Anyway, he was driving me home, and I was chewing on a stick of gum I found in his car's glove box. I remember picking a scrap of yellow paper off the car's floor. It fell when I was digging around for the gum. There were questions printed on it in black ink, which I soon read."

As with so many others, I was unaware when a big moment passed.

"By the time we reached my apartment a few minutes later, I had answered all twenty of the questions printed on the yellow paper, with a 'yes' offered to eighteen of them."

Blaine parked his new car on River Avenue, in front of my apartment, under the shade of a mature elm tree.

"After my brother turned off the engine, and before either of us moved to get out, I reported my result to him. I got eighteen out of twenty questions right on this test, I told him. And I was proud to report the score, too, as I recall. Then I asked him, what's the story on it?"

I remember him grinning when he answered.

"Turn it over, he told me, and read what's on the other side."

I did as he instructed.

"A moment later, I yelled at him. Now wait a damned minute, and I was some hot, too. Then I asked him, are you trying to tell me I'm an alcoholic?"

Even years later, I felt the rush of my teenage anger lashing out, deeply offended by such unwelcome news.

"I wasn't happy, let me tell you."

My big brother took it in stride, though he couldn't keep himself from cracking a smile.

"But in reply, my elder brother, wearing a smile, placed one of his enormous hands on my shoulder, and looked me in the eye, before saying, I'm not trying to tell you anything, my bud, you're the one who answered the questions."

As I laughed aloud at the memory, the room chuckled along with me. I'm sure many of us had scored well on that test. That might even be why it's so damned popular among people who share this illness. And right then, for just a second, I wondered how many of those questions my buddy Steve said 'yes' to when he took it.

*

"But like I told you before," I said, "there never seemed to be enough good examples around to save me from myself, you know? No way, no how, and that's for sure, eh? I was all about making my own mistakes!"

Even today, I prefer making them for myself.

"So, when my first high school girlfriend and I got serious, none of my friends were too surprised."

We met the first week of classes and got into what became a long-term thing right away.

"She was a freshman, like me, and much too young to be getting serious about stuff like that, eh?"

I shook my head at the memory.

"For me, even back then, it turned out being in love was more like taking a hostage than having a relationship, you know."

Before I got that figured out, my first love, and any that followed, ended badly.

"We gave it a good run, though, eh, and she came with me when I followed my folks to Vancouver Island a few years later. They sold the family home and moved away not long after retiring. I was still messing around with cars in those days, and there was lots of work in Montreal, and because I ran a one-man shop, I guess I might have figured there must be more money to be made out there. That was my story, back then, anyway."

That's what I told my girlfriend, and everyone else who asked.

"In truth, at the time, I had no real clue about my own, or anyone else's, business. I mean, right out of high school, my gal was already doing my taxes, eh? Business, too, not just the personal stuff."

As I recall it now, in those days, I got by, mostly, on charm. Though I still can't say if I was aware of it.

"Not only that, but me and her always shared a hankering to shake them miserable winters, you know? And no offense to my Quebecois friends, either Mon Ami. Because it was one of our dreams, and I'm talking since pretty much right after we first met, too, eh? So, when my folks started raving about life on Vancouver Island, it wasn't long before I talked her into pulling the pin on old Montreal and its cold weather!"

I nodded to the room, recalling the excitement of my first big move.

"In the end, like any geographic cure, it didn't fix my problem. In fact, once I got out to la-la-land, my drinking got worse, and fast, you know. It was like the endless summer made drinking every day make sense. For me, anyway, eh?"

I shook my head at the old memory.

"And my ex was not only devoted to me, but she was also smart, a social drinker, successful corporate salesperson, and pretty damned determined, too. Between high school and our time on the coast, she would spend most of seven lonely years trying to save me from the bottle. And I hope the man upstairs sends her the love she deserves for all that, because I didn't give it to her, and that's for sure, you know?"

A barely audible sigh, that I chose to read as one of understanding, came from the room.

"So, like I was telling you before, I got into the car business early."

My first job out of high school, at a car dealer's, soon led to me starting my own detailing and prep business.

"I got into the auto-detailing, prep, and restoring right out of high school. Back then, in Montreal, there wasn't too much competition around the Anglaise neighborhood, either, eh? So, pretty quick, I made out like a bandit, servicing the local used and new car dealerships, you know?"

Not only that, but I was popular, and within a short while after graduating from high school, did well for myself.

"But I didn't really know much about the business, eh? I guess I figured it would be the same all over, maybe? I'm not sure. Anyway, when I landed out west and set up shop, I wasn't too worried, you know?"

Soon enough, I regretted that.

"We planned our move well, thanks to my girl. She had a job waiting when we got there, and an apartment leased for us, too. As for me? Well, I grabbed a business license and leased a shop within a couple of weeks of getting off the ferry."

We moved late in the spring, and I recall the whole city looked to be in bloom when we got there.

"It was big excitement for both of us, too, at first, you know. But within a couple of weeks, it was pretty clear I'd walked into a tough market. I mean, there were three local shops doing the same thing as me, and each of them was better at it than I was, eh? Not only that, but with few local contacts, it was hard to get any of the nearby car dealers to even give me a chance."

I recall being surprised by my troubles.

"Lucky for me, or maybe not, I guess, my dad knew a guy at a big dealership in Victoria, and he convinced them to give me a try. I had to commute from our new place at Qualicum Beach, but the work was steady enough to keep the shop rent paid, and at first, it looked like I was on my way to better things there, you know."

When I remember those early days on the island, they're filled with promise. But nowadays, I know it was the guarantee of an impending disaster.

"But in business, as in life, like attracts like, you know, and the car sales racket, back then, was home to plenty of people dealing with one kind of substance abuse or another. And so, within a month of landing the contract with that Victoria car dealer, I got to know a few of their sales people a little better, if you know what I mean, eh?"

I still had plenty of the schoolboy antics up my sleeve, and liked to share them, too, once I got to know you.

"Sure enough, it didn't take me long to figure out which of them also enjoyed a drink. And because they were the ones who would keep me in detailing and prep work, I made a point of spreading the good cheer, you know."

Business, after all, is business. Or at least, that's what I told my girlfriend when she questioned the late nights.

"Because, in the early days out there, I did most of my drinking after hours, and the work didn't suffer. In fact, as I grew more popular with the sales team, business picked up. It looked like a dream coming true for a while, you know?"

It didn't last.

"Well, by the time my contract with the dealership was canceled a year and a half later, I was drinking pretty much full-time. And maybe three months after that, I was locked out of my shop for failing to pay rent. Of course, by then, they had also cut off the utilities, so there was no reason to be there anyway, eh?"

I paused, and felt again, the pain leftover from the failure of my business during that first geographic cure.

"By then, me and the girlfriend had been together better than five years, and she was running out of patience with my antics. Because she loved it out there, and despite the trouble I made at home, her career was taking off. And I might have been more than a little jealous about that, eh?"

I remember a bitter and lingering anger showing up after I got loaded.

"Did I mention not being the violent type?"

I nodded to the room.

"Well, I'm not."

Never have been, either.

"Not now, and not ever. I've never been into the tough guy routine. No sir, I'm a lover, not a fighter, and that's for sure, you know. I'm one of those guys that won't step on a spider if I can help it, eh? And, no matter how bad things got, I've always been grateful for being that way."

I mean it, too. Because, if nothing else, being a non-violent person kept me from doing physical harm to the people I loved. No matter how long I lived as a practicing alcoholic. Not only that, but since getting sober, I've made a habit of thanking the man upstairs for small miracles.

"Anyway, before I was done with it, you know, I also turned my ex's life into a kind of living hell, eh? Not with violence either, you understand. There're worse kinds of torture than that. I know because I inflicted many of them. My shrink calls the head games I liked to play back then passive aggressive."

I shook my head and paused, still embarrassed.

"But with amends to my ex-girlfriend made years ago, nowadays it's rare for me to think much about it, you know. Unless I'm sharing my story."

I grinned to the room, again pleased to be sober. The price of staying that way was telling the truth of my drinking life.

"Because, though she did her best, you know, and likely gave me far too many chances, eventually, she had to get away from me. Or, depending how you look at it, she was lucky enough to escape."

I paused a moment and recalled what Blaine had told me about love, marriage, and divorce, when at last I shared that part of my story with him.

*

"Anyhow, when I took my first geographic cure," I said, "it was for love, not to get sober."

I sipped from the water glass in my hand.

"At least, that's what I told myself. Because, despite a mountain of evidence already built up around me, I didn't think I had a problem with booze."

I replied to the room's communal nod with one of my own.

"See, I met the great love of my young life when I was fifteen, and she was about a year older. And right from the start, I figured she was it for me."

I grinned at the room.

"She was petite, with blue eyes, and curly red-hair, and the older sister to one of my good buddy's girlfriends. Pardon my gangster talk, but she was a bavishing ruby, let me tell you!"

Without thinking, I lapsed into the familiar slang of my youth. The memory of those times remains, for me, close at hand.

"So, with about one look, that girl had me, and it's no lie. And lucky for me, she had the same idea. We hit it off. Right away, too."

I remember pulling a few teen-aged break-and-enters in the company of the fellow who long ago introduced us.

"And though it wasn't my first time around the block, let me tell you, I felt things for that girl I haven't since, and that's a fact, my friends."

More slang emerged without asking me for permission. A low murmur passed through the room in reply. At least, in my mind, it did.

"But not even young love could hope to save me from myself. And she tried. Over and over, again. With kind words, good deeds, patient suffering, and feminine wiles. All wasted on the younger me."

I shook my head, and for a moment, heard the nostalgic song of lost youth. Lucky for me, I learned long ago how that stuff is nonsense.

"She did her best, too, trying to get me to see a few things, about me, and my life, but I wasn't ready to hear it."

And though I tried my best to love her, with as much as I knew then, there was too much on the wrong side of the scale to even things out between us. Decades later, we learned how to be friends.

"But she was there, in my early drinking days, and all the way, too. Not just keeping house, but working, paying the bills, and looking after me. From holding, to keeping six, and planning, she was in it, and deep. With me, and whoever I was running with, true, every time, and no doubts, never, about her. She'd have done time, and risked it more than once, to look out for me, and my crew, as well. That girl was the goods."

An ache passed through my gut. Maybe a second later, a shudder followed it.

"I will also tell you I felt neither guilt nor shame for putting her life in real danger, many times, in my thoughtless, drunken, youth. I can only be grateful to the man upstairs for watching over her, and me, too, when I couldn't."

Once again, I shook my head at the ugly memories.

"Besides, though I don't know how we made it through some

of those times alive, thanks to you and the man upstairs, I know why. And that's all that matters to me."

I smiled as a ripple of applause passed through the room. As it faded into the darkness, I went on with my story.

"See, we were a pair of ignorant, already broken kids when we first met. But neither of us knew that."

I had dropped out by then, but Deb was still going to school.

"So, we grabbed onto each other, and got stuck, like goose shit, on a blanket. Pardon the street-talk, but we were together for six months before I did my first bit at the Vaughan Street youth center at Winnipeg."

Only remembering those times brings that stuff out of me. Though I ached for Debbie every day, and night, when inside that first time.

"I'll tell you what, it was the biggest relief I knew, up to then, when I got out, to find her there, waiting for me."

I won't forget seeing her, standing across the street, framed by the pale sunlight of late fall in Manitoba, when I walked out of jail that first time. Forever after, she was the picture of freedom for me. Despite the shared prison, we soon made of our lives.

"Well, after that, I guess I never wondered about her and me again, not for quite a few years, anyhow."

Though we never married, we were soon living together, and did, off and on, until shortly before my last time in jail.

"Over the next fifteen years, she would suffer her share of the nightmares known only by the wife of a problem drinker. Plus, many of those that come with a mate who makes his way by the proceeds of crime. But she was a good and loyal partner to me, despite the misdeeds fueling my lifestyle in those days."

I stopped for another sip from the water glass.

"So, I don't really know when, but not long after I turned eighteen, the money I made from property crimes overtook the income I earned from day jobs. Not long after that, the time I spent in jail went up, too."

Though I can't remember when she first did, I know it was Debbie who pointed out the tie between jail time and easy money to me.

"Anyhow, after doing another three-month bit at Headingley Jail a few years later, I got home to find her getting ready to move out. When I asked her what was up, she told me she was moving to Calgary and planned to live with her mom. I was welcome to come along, but only if I was ready to give up the gangster's life."

Nor will I forget her many tears, shed on that Winnipeg summer afternoon.

"Well, I wasn't ready for any such thing. But I wished her the best. Before heading out to restart the party."

When I awoke, badly hungover, maybe a week later, she was gone.

"Not two weeks after that, when the rent on our Winnipeg apartment came due, I bought a one-way ticket and jumped on a Greyhound instead of paying it. Because I planned to join her at her mom's place in Calgary."

If memory serves, I might have been running from an arrest warrant, too.

"So, not long after getting to Alberta, thanks to one of her brothers, I got a full-time construction job. We made out like bandits for a while, there, living the straight life. She worked as well, and our first year out west would be our best together, maybe because we stayed mostly sober."

Our arrival synced with a seventies oil boom in Alberta. That meant jobs were plentiful, and wages there were higher than any I had seen at home. So, despite rising prices for everything, there was no need for the proceeds of crime. For the first time in years, I lived without it.

"And going straight proved easier than I thought it would. There was plenty of work, and the money was better than I remembered. If we could've stayed sober, things might have turned out real nice."

I grinned while looking out to the audience and paused a beat before hitting them with my punchline.

"But then, if I could have figured out how to stay sober without you folks, I wouldn't have a story to share with you here today."

I refilled my water glass from the melting-ice filled decanter on the table and drank a cooling sip while a ripple of applause passed through the room.

FOUR

"It took a few more years of serious drinking to split us up for good, but there were semi-regular splits to mark our progress."

By now, I understand things like choice and responsibility, but for a while, there was plenty of guilt, and shame, too.

"I no longer blame myself, either, for my ex's problems with booze and pills. Not entirely, anyhow. Because I've been at this long enough to know I'm not responsible for anyone but me. Not only that, but my life was such a mess in those days I had no time to help anybody else."

Besides, I don't remember the idea of helping anyone but me, coming up through most of those years.

"I stayed sober for almost a year, though, like I told you, when we first shacked up together at Calgary, and worked full time, too, hanging drywall with one of her brothers. But it's a progressive illness, my friends, and that's a fact. Though I didn't know it! So, even while I wasn't drinking, it was getting worse."

Our first Christmas spent there started a party that didn't end until I went back to jail.

"Not only that, but once I got started again, for the next several years, my drinking was out of control."

I remember trying to stop, more than once, too.

"In fact, most of the next few years there, by now, are something of a blur. But I know we split, or tried to, about two years later. By that time, of course, I had lost the job hanging drywall with her brother. And while I doubt one had anything to do with the other, I'm pretty sure I used it against her. Because she followed me into the abuse cycle and was already fighting her own battles with booze and pills by then."

I remember paying more attention to her troubles than

mine.

"Unless you've been there, it might be hard to see the humor, but I'm sure many of you will know what I'm talking about. After losing my day job, I spent most of my time boosting to pay for the booze and valium we used. Much of the time, we were too wiped out to function. It was your basic three-year stupor. Drunk every night, wasted on assorted pills, hating everything, but claiming to love each other. While getting in deep with the disease of addiction."

I no longer remember how often we broke up, only that, finally, we got back together one time less.

"When we finally did split, for good, fixing my broken heart took up most of my time, energy, and money. With booze, the medicine I used for it."

Nowadays, I mark that time by its many falls from grace.

"In between trips in and out of jail, that is."

I was in there too often for many of them to stand out.

"Anyhow, I went ahead and lost everything important to me, including my self-respect, during the next few years of heavy drinking, supported mainly by property crimes."

Six months after that final breakup with Deb, I took a geographic cure and moved north to the province's capital city.

"So, when I moved to Edmonton, after putting in a few months up at Fort Saskatchewan for a string of bee-and-ees pulled in Calgary, it was to make a new start. Because right around then, I decided it was time for me to give up the life of crime. I went back to hanging drywall about the same time, too. Though I was still drinking too much on most weekends."

I was gambling, too, as often as I could, but not every day, by then.

"What I remember most about those days is a near constant fear."

My fear was, at least partly, fed by recurring dreams.

"Because, instead of resting at night, in my dreams, I struggled with nightmares of a howling prairie thunderstorm and couldn't find my way home. And I couldn't figure out why, either. But on plenty of mornings, I woke up more exhausted than when I laid down."

Lack of sleep often left me with a short fuse, too.

"Anyhow, that fear was there in the morning, too, grumbling in the pit of my stomach, like I had eaten something bad."

Even then, I knew a doctor couldn't help me.

"The only thing that took it away, for any time at all, was booze."

Despite my growing misery, I held a day job for most of the first year up there after getting out of jail.

"But within a year of getting up there, a run of bad luck at a local casino got me pinched for passing a couple of bad cheques. Weekend boozing meant I was too broke for anything but a legal aid lawyer, and a cranky judge gave me another three-months in Fort Saskatchewan for my trouble."

I was sick and tired of being inside by then, but growing less immune to the program pitches that were a regular part of it.

"As usual, I went to program meetings while stuck in there, too. Because, if nothing else, they broke up the long evenings on the inside."

The utter boredom of life in jail is unmatched.

"Or maybe it was the suicide attempts that seemed to happen, no matter in which place I was locked up, that got to me. I don't know. At least, not for sure. But let me tell you, they sure happened on the regular."

None of the cons I knew, before or since, told me that stuff.

"From the earliest one, on my first night in the Vaughan Street lockup, at fifteen, when a kid, alone in the cell next to mine, hung himself. While around him, the rest of us had to listen, as he strangled his life away, in the semi-dark of those cells."

So far, I haven't been able to get the sound of it out of my head.

"To the finale, on what turned out to be my last time inside, when I held an inmate's legs, trying to keep him from choking out, as a couple of other prisoners worked to get him loose, after we found him hanging from a wet and tightly wrapped towel he tied to a pipe in the empty showers."

And every time it happened, no matter in which joint, I remember the jail guards taking their time before showing up, in response to the alarm.

"To me, killing yourself looked like a popular way to check out, for a jailbird, and maybe I didn't like being so close to it. I'm not sure. All I know is, I can't forget what the last guy said to me after we kept him from offing himself."

I paused, again replaying the long-ago nightmare scene, a forever saved movie clip, in my head.

"As he lay on the floor, and the color in his face came back, he opened his eyes, and looked at me. I was sitting next to him, exhausted and staring at his blue-red face, waiting for the medic to get there."

I nodded, more to myself than to the room, as the memory came to life in my mind.

"He looked up at me, and I guess because of his throat being hurt from trying to hang himself, he couldn't even whisper. But he tried, and that's for sure. I remember shaking my head to show I couldn't hear him. Then he moved his eyebrows a little, like he was trying to nod, to show he wanted to speak. And so, maybe to humor him, I leaned in closer."

To this day, what he said makes my blood run cold.

"Then he growled at me. Are you happy now, Blaine?"

For a moment, I was stunned.

"See, what I can't forget is how those words made me feel. Or the way I jumped away from him, with a kind of instinctive recoil, and felt for a minute like I might pass out. Even the way his eyes seemed to bulge a little, in time with his words, is still as clear as yesterday, in my mind."

But I made no reply, then.

"Only a moment later, the bulls got there, and they pushed me out of the way, and hauled him off to the infirmary. And I never saw that guy again either, because I got out of there before he did."

Neither did I care to, and that's a fact.

"Not only that, but I didn't really know him. He was an inmate in the cellblock, not a friend from outside. But maybe what he asked me after we stopped him from checking out that day helped to wake me up."

I'm not sure.

"What I know is, I went to a meeting later that night, and since, I've been going to them, steady, too."

Just then, I thought of my baby brother Travis, and how taking him to his first meeting all those years ago helped me stay sober.

*

"So," I said, "when I got to Edmonton, I sure wasn't thinking about getting sober, and that's a fact. Because, though I was on the run, right about then, there wasn't anybody too interested in chasing me down."

While my dive convinced few in attendance that night, it proved good enough for the Calgary commission to cut me a cheque. Soon after, the show's promoter happily converted it to cash.

"Instead of splitting town and making for home with the crew, after the fight card, I hung around Calgary for a while. There was an ex-girlfriend living there, and some kind of heart-broke teenage reunion might've taken place. But after taking that well-paid dive, the thing I hit hardest was the bottle. So, who can say for sure?"

I recall waking up, a week or a few mornings later, to a note on a hotel dresser. The high school ex had gone. And soon after, I was off to greener pastures.

"Because the next few weeks passed in the blur of an all-out binge, partly fueled by a lucky streak in the casinos of Cowtown that helped keep the good times rolling. Until the wow finish, it was something of a drunkard's paradise, as I recall it now."

I paused for a sip of water.

"But we've all been there, or, I should say, many of us have, and so I'll spare you the gory details of that last drunk. Let's just say, by the time I stepped off a late-arriving greyhound, the streak had ended, I was down to my last few dollars, nursing a heartache, without a roof over my head, and nowhere was the only place left to go."

I remember thinking, as I climbed onto the bus leaving Calgary, how the world had never felt so empty.

"Now today, I find the melodrama of those last days of my drinking funny, but back then, I wasn't self-aware enough to get the joke."

I laughed aloud at the memory of a self-absorbed, drunken me. Then waited while a chuckle passed through the crowd.

"And don't fret, because this isn't a romance novel I'm sharing either, so I won't be whining about that high school heartbreak."

As with most of my romances, it ended with a bang.

"See, what I hoped most just then was that my brother would offer me a bed, if not three squares a day, until I could get a few things figured out. Like where my next dollar was coming from. Or how to get my rep back, after selling it down the Bow River in Calgary. And, of course, how to deal with the flame burning for that high school ex."

What I remember most is the fear.

"I won't lie; while the teenage fire went out long ago, the shame of that dive seems likely to burn forever. And I was consumed by fear. Because by then, as much as anything else, maybe I didn't want the world to know, for sure, what a scumbag I was, I guess."

Lucky for me, I can't forget it.

"Anyway, right there, my biggest worry was that my brother might say no when I asked him for a bed."

Though I didn't tell Blaine, he watched the fight at Calgary from a ringside seat, and knew me, and the sweet science, too, well enough to see what happened.

"Because if my big brother turned me away, there wasn't enough money left in my jeans to catch the next bus out of town. And that scared me, too."

By now, what's left of most of those memories are fragments. The stuff that sticks is the way my head worked back then. Or, maybe, how it didn't. And, of course, the abundant fear.

"So, wait until you hear where my head was at before I got on that bus. And remember what I told you earlier, about my older brother being sober? I knew about it and understood he lived without the partying and kept a dry home for himself."

When attending the fights, he didn't drink.

"I don't recall him telling me about any roommates or a woman living with him, though."

He might have, just the same.

"See, before a fight, I got really focused."

Even in those days, I made an effort to train, despite increasing problems with booze.

"It was like having a case of tunnel vision that started after signing a contract and got worse until fight night."

Though a bender of varying length followed every fight.

"But afterwards, and most times pretty quick, too, I got wasted."

It turns out neither head space is good for hanging onto memories.

"So, I can't be too sure about what my big brother might have told me about his Edmonton deal before the Calgary fight happened. Or, if I asked him about it later."

When looking back, my life then appears a maelstrom, even to me.

"But it was plenty clear, despite the usual haze that seemed to disguise much of my life, from me, in those days, that staying at his place would mean not drinking. And that wasn't a happy thought, my friends, make no mistake about it. I was concerned, and had been, about that, since long before putting myself in a place where I needed to ask for help."

When he left after the first dry holiday he spent with our family at Winnipeg years earlier, I had vowed not to visit him in Alberta. To my knowledge, Blaine remained the only person I then knew who did not drink booze.

"Because, in those days, other than when training, I couldn't imagine why anyone would want to quit drinking for even a short while."

I nodded to the room in reply to a murmur of laughter.

"I also remember being quite surprised to later find out how many of the world's people lived without the stuff."

Through the unseen crowd before me, another shared chuckle passed. To me, then, booze looked to be the world's best, and maybe only, choice when it came time for making and sharing good times. And the foundation of any decent party.

"Not only that, but like I told you before, my brother had not tried to sell me on going to meetings, or even said anything about the program, to that point. He just stayed sober and went to them without preaching to anyone about it. At least, that's how it looked to me, then, as I recall it now."

Though I didn't know it, by that time he was working to help others find their own recovery.

"All the same, there was no way I wanted to be stuck in a place where I wouldn't have easy access to a bottle when I wanted it. And with or without a dollar in my pocket, my ego was still in good enough shape to kick my ass into a liquor store before heading for the bus depot in downtown Calgary."

I paused for another sip from the water glass. While recalling my shame at finding only enough cash for a mickey waiting in the pockets of those faded jeans.

"I only had enough cash to get a mickey of vodka. So, I nursed it through the trip, sneaking quick nips when in the bathroom, and chewed gum instead of eating. I left the dead soldier stuffed between my seat and the sidewall when I stumbled off the bus at Edmonton. Then, I was on my best behavior. And barely felt buzzed as I stood there in front of my big brother."

Years later, Blaine told me he knew I was drunk.

"But when I saw him standing there, it looked to me like he might have been waiting a long time for me to show up. And something about seeing him like that got to me, I guess."

I still can't say for sure.

"So, before I knew it, I was fessing up, and mooning like a lovesick calf, just the way I told it to you."

I reached again for the water glass. Then recalled the first meeting with my brother from another mother, and future roommate, Steve B., later the same night. As the water cooled my throat, I smiled at the memory.

*

"So," I said, "by the time I took a buddy's offer of a car sales job at Edmonton, even I could feel things getting out of hand, you know? On the inside, I mean. And though we were only in our early twenties, my ex was fed up with me."

For me, those early years of daily drinking led to serial infidelity.

"I mean, for a while there, the marriage of booze and charm made it pretty hard to keep my pants on, eh?"

Far too many times, I woke up not knowing who was lying next to me.

"Anyway, after what might have been our fifth or sixth infidelity-based split, I moved east, but just over the mountains, to Edmonton, Alberta, you know, where I made my last stand, as a practicing alkie."

I paused a moment, as memories threatened to flood my mind.

"Now, by then, though things were sliding, and fast, I was still prideful enough to think I had my life under control, you know. So, I was pretty sure a full-time sales job wasn't going to be a problem for me, eh? The way I had things figured, it was a soft gig that paid well, and I could easily stop the day drinking and switch to partying at night and on weekends."

When I got to Edmonton, I hadn't worked in over a calendar year.

"But I was losing confidence, and fast, in my hold on reality, in those days, too, eh? I mean, when I wasn't loaded, even thinking was getting to be pretty tough. There were times I would get so messed up I had a hard time keeping a hold on what was real and what wasn't. To where even talking could seem like too much, you know?"

On most days, I felt it might be a better idea for me to disappear.

"Only a drink, or sometimes two, made it better."

By then, I felt the need for a drink several times per day.

"Through most of the next few years, after moving to Edmonton, I rented a single room, with bath, in a west end motel. It was a flophouse, filled with derelicts and working girls, but the joint rented by the week."

When moving in, I remember telling myself it was a short-term thing.

"By then, I was no longer sure what might come out of my mouth either, in the heat of the moment, not only at work, but in casual talking."

It was getting harder for me to tell the difference between inside and outside conversations.

"Even telling the difference between when I was talking to myself, in my head, and when it was to others, in the outside world, was getting to be quite a job, too, eh?"

The only safety was sleep.

"So, for a while there, my number one concern was getting drunk enough so I could fall asleep. Because, so long as I was sleeping, nothing bad could happen. At least, nothing that would be my fault. I mean, that's what I told myself, eh?"

I was growing more desperate, but didn't yet know it.

"At the same time, it was taking more and more booze to knock me out, you know? And the sales jobs were asking more of me, too, eh? It looked like my boyish charm might be losing its appeal, and that meant I had to put in more work to close deals. Faster and faster, I remember how my life was making less and less sense to me."

Since then, I've always known what people mean when they claim to be overwhelmed by confusion.

"The longer I lived that way, the more nervous I got, and the more desperate I was to stay in my flophouse room, away from the world and its people, you know? All I wanted was to drink until falling into the restless dreams I then called sleep. Until that happened, I was content to stare at the snow playing on the little TV that came with the room."

Cable cost an extra fifteen bucks a week, and I refused to pay it.

"Most of you here probably know how it goes, and that's about how it went, too, eh? Not long after I started the first sales job, it was soon clear, to me, anyway, that dealing with people when I was sober didn't work. So, the drinking at work started with one at lunchtime, on my first day there, to steady my nerves. The next day, I had a shot with my coffee, to steady me until I could get a drink at lunchtime. At first, one seemed enough to get me through the afternoon. A glass of wine after dinner on Friday, at the end of my first week, to celebrate some early success, also seemed a good idea, you know. But a couple of days later, when I showed up for work, bright and early, I was slobbering drunk, at eight o'clock on Monday morning, eh."

Not two hours after that, I was looking for a new job.

"Like I told you before, though, charm was my calling card, and while selling didn't come natural to me, it was low-effort work, which suited my declining health. Not only that, but I told myself I was better at it than detailing cars, you know."

The daily drinking, by then, and unknown to me, had put me on shaky ground.

"For another year or two, I burned my way through a sales job of one kind or another every few months, with cars, encyclopedias, furniture, steak knives, and vacuum cleaners among many stops that paid the motel room rent. I was plastered most of the time, you know? And pretending to nurse a broken heart, so I had an excuse for it, eh?"

Sadly, driving while drunk became a habit.

"But there is no excuse, you know, for drinking and driving. Not then, now, or ever. And I was lucky to get caught before the courts really cracked down on it. Otherwise, who knows if I'd even be here to share my story with you today."

I don't remember committing the crime that got me thrown

into a detox center for thirty days of treatment.

"Anyway, one day, after several drinks with lunch, and on the way back to work, I ended up driving my dealership loaner car into a restaurant's lobby, you know. Shortly after that, the legal system took care of the rest."

As the largest part of my sentence, the judge demanded I get treatment for substance abuse.

"It wasn't my first offence, but fortunately, nobody was hurt, and so, instead of jail and a record, the judge gave me a fine and thirty days in a local treatment center. And, like it or not, they forced me to go to my first meetings while an inmate there, eh?"

I went but wasn't moved.

"So, when I got out, after getting back to that room in the west end flophouse, my first purchase was two bottles from the liquor store next to the lobby. And when I came up for air two days later, it wasn't to go looking for a meeting, either, you know."

My thirtieth birthday passed on that long-lost weekend.

"Because it's true what folks say, how if you live next door to a toilet long enough, you eventually get used to the smell."

I didn't even notice the stench of the one in which I was living.

"So, when the sour taste of a hangover woke me that Monday morning, it seemed a day like any other, and I was no more pleased than usual to greet it. I remember the same want for a drink of something, to calm the ever-present jumble of scary thoughts filling what passed for my mind, was the number one concern."

After pulling a newspaper from a pile on the lobby desk, I instead grabbed a coffee from the machine in the hallway on the way back to my room.

"Thanks to the want ads, by the time my first vending machine coffee was gone I had lined up a couple of places looking for sales help, eh? After a shower, I planned to see about getting myself back to work."

To apply for the sales job topping my list meant going

downtown, and despite my circumstances, I was not only still vain, but arrogant as well.

"Anyway, it turned into a long morning, with plenty of walking. Because I applied for a couple of different jobs, and was hungry, and in a bit of a daze, just before noon, and nursing quite a nasty hangover, too, by then. So, when I saw people walking into what looked like a restaurant, I followed them inside, eh? And right away, before I could really check the place out, some fellow pointed me to a pot of self-serve coffee, and I grabbed myself a cup of it, you know."

My hand shook as I added milk and sugar to a Styrofoam cup.

"Before I could find a table, someone called out time, from somewhere unseen, and just like that, everyone in the room seemed to rise from their seats, together, as one, and moved towards where I was standing, you know. For a minute, I just about panicked, eh? Then, I glanced over my shoulder, and there were stairs behind me, and when I looked back, the same fellow who pointed out the coffee pot was at my side, and nodding to me, with a reassuring smile, as he took my elbow and turned me towards them."

While not a stampede, the people wasted no time in making for the stairway.

"And so, with no chance to argue, I was soon walking along with an assembling crowd, down the stairs and into a large, carpeted room, with a high ceiling, filled with a dozen or more rows of folding chairs, you know. At the far end, a dais waited, and behind it stood a middle-aged woman, who smiled a greeting to me while the unknown friend led us to a pair of seats near one end of the front row."

Though not yet sure of what might come next, I remember not expecting any lunch to be served.

"A few minutes later, though I could have left at any time, I sat through my first program meeting held outside a treatment center."

FIVE

"By then, maybe I was just sick and tired of being that way, you know? I mean, either that, or it's just like the old timer's say, and everybody hears this thing when they're ready to, and not a minute before, eh."

I nodded at the people in front of me.

"Who can say? I can't. Not for sure, anyway. And I doubt I'll ever be able to, either. But it doesn't bother me. Because I turned all that stuff, and everything else, too, over to the man upstairs a long time ago."

I paused for a sip of water as a murmur of approval passed through the room.

"Anyway, it turned out the downtown club was not only home to a daily noon meeting but hosted morning, afternoon, and evening groups as well, eh? So, when the early crowd left, I stuck around and ordered myself a light lunch. Not long after I finished eating, somebody made the same call, and before I knew it, I was sitting and listening to another meeting, this one with fewer people in the room."

At the time, there was no reason to argue with anyone over what I heard while attending them, either.

"After the second one, though, I remember going into a kind of trance. I was shaking a little, and sweating a lot, but didn't want to leave that club."

Indeed, even after the second meeting, for reasons unknown to me, I hung around the place, drinking free coffee.

"Another meeting happened a couple of hours later, and I went to that one, too. Then I had dinner, but didn't eat much, because my gut turned from drinking free coffee. I was craving a drink, too, by then, you know?"

The need for a drink was strong, but something else made me stay. And I still don't know what it was.

"But like I told you, I was in no hurry to leave. And so, by about nine that night, I had sat through four program meetings."

Though I didn't say a word in those meetings that day, the people working there, and attending the club, welcomed me sticking around the place.

"That club, and the people, made quite an impression on me. And right away, too. I remember wanting what a lot of them seemed to have. Because, through that day, I met several of them, too, eh? And jeeze, it sure seemed like everybody wanted to meet me and shake my hand."

Though I didn't know why.

"And though I didn't know why that was, it had been so long since people were glad to see me; I wasn't going to argue with them about it, you know?"

I was a newcomer but didn't know it.

"Because I didn't even know what a newcomer was, then."

My sponsor later told me.

"Anyway, it took a few tries before anything stuck with me, you know. Because I went back to my hotel room and drank enough to knock myself out later that same night. Then I was in and out for another few months, and cracking up, until getting more than a few days of dry time together, eh?"

My last months of drinking are mostly a blur.

"And something must have told me it was my time, you know? Though I can't tell you for sure, who or what it might have been. But I'm one of them gee-o-dee types now, so you know what I think, eh?"

While many have their doubts, I'm a true believer.

"And lucky for me, the door to that club swings both ways."

I kept coming back there, no matter how many times I went and got drunk after sitting through a program meeting.

"See, the people there always welcomed me back, no matter how many times I went out for more drinking. Not only that, but somebody there gave me a piece of good advice, and though I can't remember who it was, for a change, I took it, you know? So, one day, after about six months of hanging around and trying to figure things out on my own, I asked one of the men at that club to help me get sober."

The fellow became my program sponsor and remains so to this day.

"He was a guy I heard speak at one of the noon meetings that got to be a habit of mine in those days."

People I met at the club told me he was an old school program guy. Others told me he was just what I needed.

"Now, in those days, heartbreak was still a big part of my claim to fame, and I also liked to tell folks it fed my drinking, you know. When questioned about it, I would trot out the tale of my lost high school love to explain my stinkin' thinkin', and then blame her, along with my broken heart, for whatever didn't work in my life, eh."

As I remember it now, heartbreak was among the most versatile of my crutches.

"But more than a few people I knew around the club told me this guy was different, and it wasn't long before he showed me what they meant, too, you know."

Oh boy, did he show me!

"Anyway, I met him one day at the club, and we hit it off right away, too, eh? It was as if he knew me, or we had chemistry between us, or something."

Though I didn't know what difference it could make, I was growing desperate, and wanted a program sponsor.

"So, because people were telling me I needed one, only a few hours after we met, I asked him to be my sponsor."

I didn't know it, but he had heard me tell my story.

"To my surprise, he said yes!"

Even then, to me and my addled brain, he looked to be a good fit.

"So, we started hanging around together, you know? And not just at the club, either. Because even me, still dazed and often hungover, could see he had something different going on, eh?

Anyway, the day after meeting him, he started taking me with him to meetings around the city, picking me up and driving me home afterwards."

In my head, I did my best impression of a guy trying to get sober.

"I can't explain it. But to me, he seemed like a brother, or an old, but close friend, right away, and not just a program sponsor, eh?"

He still does, too.

"So, one evening, two weeks later and after another program meeting, which we were going to five or six a week, by then, he showed me how it was going to be. If I wanted to get what he had, eh?"

I remember bitching to him over something long forgotten when he showed me what he meant. Because in those days, my habit was to take the blame for little that happened in my life. Or anyone else's.

"So, there we are, sitting at a booth in a west end Edmonton chain restaurant one night after a meeting, you know."

We went for coffee together after most program meetings in those days.

"And I'm bellyaching about losing my latest job, being unhappy with the current girlfriend, living in a flophouse, and not being able to stay sober because of it, to this man, who is now my program sponsor, eh?"

In memory, my ego was on a roll that night.

"Maybe I didn't have a hangover for a change, or was even dry a week or two by then, but I'm no longer sure."

I don't remember a word of what I blathered to Blaine. But I hope never to forget his response to it.

"Now, as I recall, my sponsor didn't even grunt in reply. Not at first. But he sat and listened, looking at me with concern, as I spilled more of the same old bile onto the table between us there, eh? I mean, he looked so concerned, more than once, I thought he might cry, you know?"

I need not have worried.

"Then, after letting me vent, he took a deep breath, and shook his head, slow, like he was in deep thought, and pondering, before he replied."

I thought my plan had worked.

"I remember thinking I had him right where I wanted him, you know?"

Then he spoke.

"So, then he looks across the table at me, and he says, well Steve, those are some real troubles you've got there, and that's for sure. Then he stopped, for just a minute, eh, and looked at me, hard, like, before he speaks again."

On his face, there was no sign of tears.

"For a second, or maybe longer, I was a little scared, because my new sponsor no longer looked like he wanted to cry, eh?"

In those days, we didn't yet know each other well.

"Did I tell you he was a burly construction worker when I met him? He was maybe mid or late-thirties, I think, with a big personality to go with it, too, you know. And what about his Indigenous heritage? Did I say anything about that? Well, he was up front about that, too. And maybe even kind of militant about it, eh? I mean, that's how it was to me, anyway, when I was first getting to know him."

He was handsome, with dark eyes, light brown skin, and thick black hair, with curls falling to an always starched shirt collar. He most often wore a no-nonsense look on that face, too. But he showed little from behind those impassive but sharply inquisitive eyes. I recall thinking how glad I was not to have met Blaine in his drinking days.

"I can still remember how the hair on the back of my neck stood up a little, and the way my gut got tight, when he sat there quiet like that."

Only a second or two passed before he spoke.

"So, a moment later when he cleared his throat, and then grinned at me, I relaxed. But I remember thinking how he seemed to have made up his mind about something, eh?"

I was right.

"Anyway, what my sponsor told me next, well, it changed my life, you know."

I sipped from the water glass, wanting to get it straight in my head before sharing the short but well-remembered scene with them.

"He started by telling me, Steve, I'm gonna say this once, and not again, so listen close, if you're ready to get sober."

I remember the tightness in my gut getting worse, but recall nodding to show he had my attention.

"Then he stopped and looked at me, quiet, for a second, you know. He stared at me, before saying, in a deadpan voice, Steve, there's only two things you gotta do, and that's don't drink, and go to meetings."

He paused, and stared at me again, for several more seconds.

"Then, he gave me that look again, the hard one, you know? And maybe a second or two later, he goes, in the same voice, now stop wasting my time, and yours."

A smile passed across my lips.

"I hope I never forget the way he looked at me across the table that night. Because he was deadly serious, and lucky for me, I knew it."

I nodded and recalled Blaine's words before repeating them.

"Then, he growled at me one more time. Because to me, in that moment, he was a bear, sitting across from me, you know? So, he growls, now, quit blaming that bullshit heartbreak story for your troubles and get busy reading the book."

The look. I've never forgotten it.

"After fixing me with another unfriendly stare, he finishes up by telling me, and Steve, if you wanna keep hangin' around with me, that's the way it's got to be, and I don't want to hear another word about it."

I remember how, in the next moment, blood rushed from the rest of my body and collected in my gut, and feeling that I might faint.

"Maybe his plain talk shocked me, eh? Or maybe it was just my time. I don't know. But for whatever reason, his words cut through the fog filling my brain in those days, you know?"

Not only that, but something told me he meant every one of them.

"Anyway, for a change, I didn't get mad at him, like I did everyone else back then, for setting me straight, either, eh?"

Something happened to me there, but I don't know what it was.

"Or maybe it's like the old timer's say."

Many of us have heard them.

"That only when a student is willing does the teacher appear."

Nowadays, I accept those words as gospel.

"Anyway, I know something he told me got to me that night, and for sure, eh? Though I can't tell you what it was, or how it got there, either. All I know is, since that night, I haven't had to drink a single drop of booze."

As if on cue, I thought of my buddy Travis, and the mental gymnastics he later went through because of that same old school sponsor.

*

"So, when I got off that bus," I said, "it was plain enough to my elder brother that I was in dire straits."

A few months after I got sober, he told me he believed it was that way for a while.

"I know that because, later on, he told me about it."

Though he said nothing at the time.

"But to spare my giant ego, and avoid making me mad, he said nothing about it, then. And the next morning, the only thing I could think about when I woke up was the hangover waiting for me."

Even before I opened my eyes, a slow throbbing began from an unseen edge of my pickled brain. Soon, if I were to avoid the worst of it, my need for a drink was going to turn from abstract to real.

We stopped for nothing but drive-thru coffee on the way to my brother's place.

"Because the night before, after grabbing my duffel bag from the bus driver and finding his car, we stopped only for a cup of drive-thru coffee. My brother didn't offer to buy me anything stronger to drink, either."

I knew better than to ask.

"Right after grabbing that coffee, I gave him the nickel tour of my affairs. Almost at once, he told me I was welcome to stay at his place. Then, he told me he had a roommate, and mentioned the no-booze policy they kept at their shared apartment."

I recall how my relief at having a place to stay was tempered by the prospect of hanging out in a booze-free home. The idea did not thrill me.

"I met his roommate, who was another sober drunk, and his best friend, according to my brother, when we got to their place."

As most people did, I near at once hit it off with Steve.

"His roommate turned out to be a tall white guy with blonde hair, who wore glasses and was a sharp dresser. He was good looking, too. And, like my brother and myself, he had a taste for the ladies."

Steve showed his gift of gab right away, charming me in a few words.

"That was soon plain, too, because despite the hour, he was on his way out to meet a woman when we got there that night."

I remember thinking hanging out with the two of them might not be so bad.

"So, when my brother burst into the spare bedroom early the next morning, where I had crashed, and told me we were celebrating his roomie's birthday with a restaurant brunch, I was, at first, pleased."

Despite the early wake-up call.

"Because I figured it meant I'd soon be grabbing a cocktail at a decent restaurant."

The happy thought of postponing my encroaching hangover at once relieved a nascent, but fast-rising, fear.

"I recall thoughts of an ice-cold Caesar, blood-red, with a crisp stalk of fresh celery, filling my head. Thus, well-motivated, it wasn't long before I was out of the shower and ready to go, friends."

When I landed in the downstairs kitchen, brother Blaine handed me a cup of fresh-brewed coffee and a slice of lightly buttered toast, and the combo settled my gut.

"A few minutes later, after a quick bite and a cup of sweet coffee, I jumped into the passenger seat of my brother's late-model domestic car, and we followed his roomie, in a black import, first to the end of the block, and then west after he turned onto Stony Plain Road."

It was my first visit to Edmonton, and I was soon lost.

"All I can remember, now, are the vast open spaces of a sprawling city, and the way its blue sky gave me an early start on the road to what was sure to be a nasty hangover."

The dark glasses I wore, a habit even then, were my only defense against the relentless power of nature.

"Somehow, a roundabout freeway trip over too many bridges and a wide river's valley ended with us on the other side of it, not fifteen minutes later."

To me, the place looked designed to confuse either locals or visitors. I remember thinking how it might be impossible to find my way back to Blaine's place as we crossed the prairie version of an urban metropolis.

"But sadly, my brother told me we had a stop to make before heading to the restaurant to eat."

Even now, I can only wonder if the endless blue sky on that Alberta spring morning relieved my concern. Because I still recall my lack of worry, there, in a strange place and under my brother's control, with a hangover on the rise, despite not knowing what might come next.

"Then he pulled off Whyte Avenue, and parked behind his roommate, on the side street, maybe a block from the corner. Before he got out of the car, he asked me to follow him, and I said ok. But when I stepped onto the sidewalk, the first thing I noticed was the neon sign of a hotel's saloon flashing at me from across a set of railway tracks."

If not for my empty pockets, I'd have left Blaine and Steve right there.

"And I didn't have the entry fee, friends, or it's a sure thing I'd have split with the boys then, and that's a fact."

In the long-ago moment, I still recall the urge coming over me.

"I remember beads of sweat forming on my brow as we walked, those two abreast and me a pace or two behind them, under a canopy of large trees lining the boulevard, back towards the busy avenue. And my nerves jangled as thoughts of the hangover waiting, maybe an hour or two away, grew. Soon, unless I got something to stave it off, I knew things were surely going to get much worse."

I was not a fan of hangovers and recall knowing how only drinking more could cheat the one waiting for me then.

"Not only that, but the sight of that saloon sign only a block away sure made the growing need more urgent."

As I thought of the long-ago moment, I recalled the way sweat covered my body, and a chill passed through me.

"A minute or two later, at the back entrance to a large three-story red brick building on the corner, they stopped. I remember an urge to run away coming over me for an instant, like there was something to be afraid of waiting for me inside. But before I could move, my brother opened a door for his roommate, and held it for me to enter."

Inside, there was a steep set of stairs. I followed Steve, first up them, and then right along a lengthy hallway on the second floor.

My gut was knotted tight, while an unknown fear gripped me.

"After I followed his roomie to the second floor, we walked into a big room, where I saw maybe sixty people milling around, and what looked to be an early morning party was underway. I was relieved and excited, too, and looked around for the bar. Either that, or a waitress, or whoever might be selling booze."

The thought of having a drink gave me a rush of relief, as I recall.

"A moment later, my brother nudged my elbow, and nodded for me to follow, which, of course, I did. He led me to a hallway, where there was a countertop cut into a wall, and people lined up, clearly waiting to place an order, or be served. At once, I relaxed, and thought of what might be on the menu."

To that point, because I saw only mugs in the hands of people filling the place, I thought it was an unlicensed speakeasy.

"When it was our turn at the window, my brother ordered for both of us, and when two steaming mugs of black coffee arrived, he made no attempt to pay. Instead, he thanked the man behind the counter and gave me a wink, before nodding for me to follow him. At a table a few feet down the hall from where we got the coffee, I found only sugar or powdered whitener to add to it. After that, I trailed him to a pair of seats near the back of the room we earlier left. Oh, and to say the least, I was crestfallen."

I paused a moment to sip from the water glass.

"It was just my luck, too, that from my seat, which was nearest the window, I could see the saloon, only a block away, I spotted when we parked. And there, above a door almost in line with the chair on which I sat, a pastel green neon sign taunted me. Like a metronome with the sound turned off, it steadily blinked. Like a toothache, it throbbed at me from the distance. And no matter where I looked, it didn't leave my mind."

The sign was a magnet to my eyes.

"Lucky for me, less than a minute later, someone closed the room's vertical blinds, and hid the damned thing."

For me, the emotional relief of no longer seeing the sign flash was palpable.

"By then, the seats in the place were filling, and my brother had told me his roomie was the man of the hour, and this 'birthday party' was the scene of the crime. I was, of course, baffled by the idea of a party without booze. But without the means to get myself out of the place, it made no sense to complain, so I didn't."

That group's monthly sober birthday party for members will

forever be my first program meeting.

"So, what happened next was their regular monthly deal, and my brother's roommate got a three-year pin that day, I think, while others celebrated being sober for one, two, five, ten, and twenty-five years."

I remember being astounded as Blaine filled me in on the details, in a whisper, between the celebrations.

"Let me tell you, my friends, in my life, I have only rarely been more impressed than I was on that morning. For, never had I been in the company of what seemed a happier group of people, and certainly not one so pleased to be sober. In fact, throughout the couple of hours we were there, I searched, in vain, for some sign of booze, or dope, to explain their shared happiness."

Of course, there was nothing to be found.

"And to me, it was a natural response. After all, how could I not be strongly impressed by what they showed me that morning? Because it was so different from anything I had experienced, drunk, or sober, before it. And even though I had to look past the angry face of a coming whopper of a hangover to do it, I saw something there, in the faces of those people, that I wanted for myself."

Though, at the time, I didn't know it.

"I remember thinking how many of them looked to be sharing a secret. But not hiding it at all well. Because they were excited to share it. In short, though I didn't know what they might be high on, they sure seemed to like it, and plenty, too."

Then, I remember thinking how what they had most resembled freedom. But, before telling any more of it, I thought of my brother Blaine, and the struggle he faced seeking a different liberty, unknown to me.

*

"See, when or if taking any kind of geographic cure back then," I said, "it was sure to include a new name and a family history to go with it. Whether it was for a gambling run, a crime spree, or a holiday after a good score, I made myself into a new man on the road."

In those days, my self-hate knew few bounds.

"But, as you can see, the color of my skin limits the options, as far as hiding in plain sight goes."

When in need of a cheap laugh on short notice, I tell people my tan is permanent. So, as usual in such moments, I waited for a chuckle to pass through the room before again speaking.

"Anyhow, and lucky for me, if I keep out of the sun, thanks to an unknown colonial ancestor, this curly hair lets me claim several backgrounds. Not only that, but to me, any of them were easier for people to deal with than my Indigenous heritage."

Because of it, road trips and holidays were big favorites during my drinking days.

"Most of the time, depending on the company I was keeping, when meeting new people, I would claim to be Italian. When gambling, I was sometimes Greek, while at other times, like on holidays, I would be Spanish. I was, sometimes, mistaken for being Mexican, and when I was, didn't deny it."

Though aside from English, the only foreign language I know is Pig Latin.

"So, by my early twenties, I had learned how to say hello, goodbye, thank you, and how to order a drink, in broken versions of what I claimed were those languages. And I told myself it was close enough to fool anyone but a native."

It wasn't.

"Only among family, or in western Canada's jails, where I was known, and well, too, did I live as myself."

Most people in Canada's prison system, then and now, were or are Indigenous.

"Because, in jail, in Canada, being Indigenous means you're in the majority."

In a Manitoba jail, I first heard the facts of my culture.

"And believe it or not, inside one of Canada's jails is also the place where I first heard stories of my Indigenous culture, and the heritage stolen from me by colonialism."

Later, in an Alberta jail, I listened while sober Indigenous inmates spoke the history of this land before it was called

Canada.

"But now isn't the time for talking about that stuff. Because what I want you to know is, when I first started going to meetings on the outside, I claimed to be Italian. In fact, after six months dry, I was still doing it."

It took an experience worth sharing to make me confront the source of my not-so-secret shame.

"And who knows how long it might have taken me to get honest about it on my own? All I know is, one day, a guy I never thought I'd see again showed up at the sober club in downtown Edmonton. Though at first, I didn't remember his face. Because at the time, he was just another alkie telling his story at the noon meeting."

What surprised me was recognizing myself playing a part in it.

"The fellow told a harrowing tale of a misspent youth, and early times in jail, where an Indigenous kid tormented and repeatedly shamed him. He talked of a burning desire for revenge on that fellow, and how it later drove him to drink, and spoiled whatever success he found in life."

The longer he spoke, the more familiar his face became to me.

"But when his story turned to recovery, after a while, he told of the need to find that fellow, and not to take revenge, but to thank him. Right about there, I figured out who he was."

It was the white boy with too many teeth, who I had beaten in the Reform School cells so many years ago.

"It was the kid from the youth detention center I told you about earlier, and I was concerned at first, and for good reason, too. See, he was a full-grown man by then and looked like he might be a handful if revenge was on his mind."

Remember, too, that I was only six months sober myself, then. The worst street habits still lived in me.

"To me, there was no way around it. If I was going to stay sober, I needed to get honest with the guy. And, only six months sober, maybe I believed the club was my turf. Anyhow, when the meeting ended, not knowing what might happen because of it, I walked up to the podium and introduced myself."

I remember being ready for trouble, but not wanting any.

"By the way, I said to the guy, if you're still looking for him, I'm the Indigenous kid who gave you all that trouble way back when."

At once, he smiled, flashing too many teeth, and looked as though he just won a prize.

"To say what happened next surprised me would be an understatement."

He was more than pleased to again meet me and said so while shaking my hand. In less than a minute, I knew he was sincere, too.

"Because our reunion was more like those shared by a pair of childhood buddies than a couple of jailhouse enemies."

Even now, I can remember relief flooding through me.

"Boy, was I ever relieved! A few minutes later, he insisted we grab a coffee, and soon joined me at a table upstairs, where he proceeded to blame me for getting him sober."

We spent the next couple of hours getting to know each other.

"Did I tell you how this program forever amazes me? Well, I was shocked to find out me and that guy had a lot in common besides jail. And though only a year into it by then, he wanted me to know what happened between us played a big part in him getting sober."

I paused for a sip from the water glass.

"Now, as far as I'm concerned, that's more of the magic of this program, what happened there, between him and me. Because you see, instead of running into an enemy from my jailhouse days as I had worried, he would soon be one of my best friends. Either in or out of the program."

I nodded, more to myself than the room, while a favorite memory filled my head. I waited for its warm comfort to embrace me before speaking.

"Not only that, but later on the same night, at a meeting

we attended together, for the first time, I spoke about my Indigenous heritage."

I don't know why.

"Though I can't tell you why I did it. Maybe it was because he was there with me? Because he knew who I was. Perhaps I didn't want him thinking less of me? Or maybe it was something completely different."

By now, I'm sure I'll never find out, and that's ok with me.

"What I know is this, my friends."

I looked out to the room before speaking.

"Since that day, I've never again felt either a need or a want to be anyone but who I am, an Indigenous man, living sober, in a world made for all of us, by the man upstairs."

SIX

"Not only that, but I've been trying to give away what I found here since about the day after I got it. Because that's the only way to keep it. At least, that's what the people who shared it with me said. When they were giving away what they had. So, I could have it. They also told me doing that was the only way they got to keep it."

At first, I didn't get the math.

"But don't get the wrong idea, because when I got here, I wasn't ready for anything more complicated than don't drink, go to meetings, and read the book."

For a while, though I didn't read much, I held fast to the first two.

"At first, and many times, even that seemed like too much."

To me, sober life was a white-knuckle experience, in those days.

"Fake it 'til you make it. That was the story of my first year. I hung around meeting rooms seven days a week, not drinking, but not really sober either. Just dry, and most of you know how that goes."

After a couple of dry months hanging around the meeting room, old timers started telling me I'd get drunk if I didn't get to work on the steps.

"Lucky for me, for at least six months, the fear of drinking was enough to keep me from slipping back into it. And by then, a group of old timers at the club, known for their old-fashioned reading of the book, told me I better get busy taking the steps if I planned to stay sober."

I wanted what they had, too.

"Fear of booze drove me, more than anything else, in those

early days."

Because getting drunk meant going back to jail, and I didn't want any more of that.

"Anyhow, maybe faking it might have been what saved me, early on, I don't know."

Even then, I didn't care.

"But, by the time I got my second program birthday cake, with a lot of help from a patient sponsor, and a loving home group, I'd made it through all twelve steps."

Though now a long time ago, I'll never forget the joy of making it through them the first time.

"The mental, emotional, and spiritual freedom I found because of taking them is so far beyond anything else that I can't compare it. What I can say is, my obsession to drink was relieved by them, and I have since lived sober."

Which is different from living dry. I paused a moment and waited for the round of applause to end.

"But like it does for many of us, clearing the wreckage of my past took a while, even with me no longer drinking. Not too long after getting out of jail, though, like I told you before, I went back to work, hanging drywall. I also started going to meetings every day. And I remember noticing, not right away, but even before I thought about taking the steps, how much better my life was when I didn't drink."

I recall being stunned by how much money there was, leftover, on paydays, despite giving up crime, too.

"But old timers in the program, who I seemed to run into a lot in those days, made it clear to me that if I wanted to stay sober, I had to give away what I had. And when I told one of them, before a meeting, that I didn't know what that meant, he just nodded, and asked me what I was doing afterwards."

I remember having no plans.

"Maybe I might have told him about a TV show, or something goofy like that, but I'm no longer sure. Anyhow, he asked me to go with him on a service call, and without knowing what that was, I agreed."

Though I didn't know it, a glimpse of my future career showed itself for the first time later that night.

"Maybe a couple of hours after the meeting ended, on a program service call to a north side flophouse, a desperate alcoholic, strung out and stinking of a fear I knew too well, would really only talk to me, the least sober of the men sent to help him."

I still remember a sensation passing through me that night, for the first time, maybe, as though I was being pulled.

"And there was a feeling I got sitting there with that guy, like I was being pulled somewhere. Maybe it's the first time I remember feeling it. But I didn't give it too much thought that night and went back to hanging drywall the next morning. I also remember thinking how I didn't want to do any more of those service calls if I could avoid them."

In those days, I was still, in my mind, newly sober.

"Not only that, but work was steady, and money was good. So, I had little interest in rocking my newly sober boat."

Barely able to help myself for so long, that I might be able to help anyone else didn't occur to me.

"And here comes another story about what I like to call the magic of this program, going to work in my life."

To me, that magic made the life I live today.

"Because, at a meeting on Thursday evening of the next week, that old timer asked me for help of a different kind. He offered me a part-time job. At a local detox center. That started on Friday at midnight."

For both of us, it was a gamble.

"Maybe I was scared to disappoint him? Or maybe I just wanted the extra money? I'm no longer sure."

I never will be, either.

"What I know is, I started work on the night shift as a counselor's helper at a treatment center northwest of St. Albert that weekend."

I jumped into it without doing too much thinking.

"Where I played the role of glorified bouncer, which

amounted to staying awake overnight with a couple of real counselors, while they were babysitting a bunch of addicts."

Unknown to me, the job came with training.

"But working there meant I had to take company-paid training in a bunch of different stuff, all new to me, including data entry, records management, and basic computer skills. Which I did, and right away, too, as I recall."

Much to my surprise, I enjoyed the evenings spent in a classroom.

"By the way, that old timer was not only my boss, but my program sponsor."

I paused a moment as a chuckle passed through the room.

"So, when I started working there, he also encouraged me, right away, to take a look at opportunities in the field."

Not wanting to argue with him, I did as he asked.

"Only a few months later, I was taking an adult-ed social work program in a community college classroom a couple of evenings a week, on the company dime, and putting in a few night shifts at the center every weekend. Not only that, but to my surprise, I enjoyed the schooling, and liked the work, too."

Only a year after that, my life again changed in a big way.

"So, a year later, after I earned my first certificate, the old timer, who was also director of that place, offered me a full-time job as an entry-level addiction counselor."

Two weeks later, I left the trades.

"In my early thirties by then, getting out of the trades seemed like a good idea, and like I said, I enjoyed the training, and even the little work I had done to that point, a lot more than swinging a hammer."

The more I worked with people, the stronger that pulling sensation became, too.

"Anyhow, imagine my surprise, when, after four years in the program, and getting through the steps, I was rewarded with a new career and a rebuilt life. I was pretty sure things couldn't get any better, friends."

The book made promises. By sticking to the program, they

came true for me.

"But you know what they say about life and making plans."

Soon, I met a fellow who helped me take another big step in recovery.

"Because passing it on is not only what keeps me sober, but it's also what keeps this thing going!"

When I met the guy, he looked barely suited to roommate duty. And he sure wasn't ready to be anybody's best friend.

"So, when I met the first guy I sponsored in this program, he was standing in the hallway of that sober club downtown, quietly checking sublet postings on one of the bulletin boards."

With my life improving, I found a taste for its comforts returned, too.

"I didn't have a listing there but was in the market for a roommate."

I had not, by then, sponsored anyone myself.

"And so, when I saw him checking rental listings at the club downtown, I walked over and said hello."

I didn't know it, but he was there looking for me.

"Only a few minutes later, he agreed to drop by for a coffee and a look at my current place, after we both went to the noon meeting."

I paused a moment and recalled my first look at the six-foot two-inch Steve B., rail thin, clean-shaven, with chiseled Caucasian features, a thick head of curly blonde hair, and dressed in typical, for him, flamboyant style.

"Even struggling to stay dry, as he plainly was the day we met, he was a sharp guy, tall and good looking, too, who stood out in a crowd. And later, when he asked me to sponsor him, I felt that weird pulling thing, and again without thinking about it, said yes."

Though it wasn't the first time someone asked me to sponsor them, it was the first time I agreed to do it. And, strangely enough, there was no hesitation, either. I said OK to Steve, on the spot.

He liked my apartment, too.

"Maybe six weeks after that, we moved into a place together, as roomies."

We agreed to split the rent of a downtown Edmonton apartment. Then lived together as sober roommates for the next several years.

"Soon, we were close friends, too. Still are! And sponsoring him is one of the greatest gifts I've ever got from this amazing program."

I'm still astounded by the paradox.

"Because sponsoring someone is to live another of the great paradoxes of our program. You see, you start out doing it to help someone else get sober, but it ends up helping you stay that way. And most times, you get more help than you give, too."

That's sure how it looks to me, anyhow, and I can only share my experience.

"I encourage you to try it. Because few things help a person stay sober more than working with other people trying to get that way. That's what being a sponsor showed me, friends, and that's for sure."

I paused as another ripple of applause passed through the room. The memory of those times loomed close.

"Anyhow, next, I'm going to share another of the confounding miracles of this program with you."

It's a favorite story of mine, too.

"See, I was already in the program for seven years, the night my younger brother got to Edmonton. And I was sharing a place with the fellow I just told you about by then. In those days, we lived in a three-bedroom apartment in a west Edmonton four-plex."

I remember being glad for the spare bedroom when my brother asked for help.

"Not only that, but both me and my roommate worked in the social work field in those days and staying sober by helping others was a lifestyle."

I remember being relieved my roomie was there. Because it meant I wouldn't be alone trying to help my younger brother. I knew that without even asking my roommate, and by then best friend.

But even after so many years, I still haven't forgotten how beaten Travis looked the night he got to Edmonton. Standing there, the better part of drunk, beneath the dull yellow of those bus terminal lights.

*

"So, after that meeting," I said, "when my brother and his roommate took me for brunch at a chain restaurant on Calgary Trail, I was still confused. On the way there, I remember my head was full of questions, too."

I recall a waitress bringing a couple of carafes filled with coffee to our table, unasked. She then shared a familiar laugh with the two men.

"And once we got into a booth, I started in on both of them about the meeting deal. They were happy enough to share answers, and took turns doing so, with a smile, between bites of an enormous meal. While also downing what seemed to be endless cups of heavily sweetened coffee, as I recollect it now."

With no booze in sight, I remember following suit. And being sad when nobody offered me anything stronger. By then, I knew better than to ask.

"I was shocked to find out my brother was already sober for seven years, and greatly impressed by his roommate's three-year stretch. Of course, I also made sure to ask them how long they planned to stay that way."

Their long-ago shared laughter was soon recalled by that of the room. I grinned and waited for it to end before again speaking.

"After they were done laughing, each of them told me he hoped to never drink again, and I remember being stunned."

To me, back then, that idea was foreign, as though it might have come from outer space, or the backward days of history.

"Because I couldn't even imagine a world without booze in those days!"

Or worse, from an unknown but terrible future, where free

will and individual freedom no longer existed.

"Both of them also reassured me, and several times, too, that they were serious about it. Not only that, but they seemed happy as a couple of pigs in you-know-what to feel that way. Pardon my language."

I recall a growing sense of bewilderment. Or at least, what I then thought that feeling might be.

"I remember being unconvinced, all the same, but kept it to myself, and tried to enjoy the free lunch."

The food, though not remarkable, kept the hangover at bay.

"From the restaurant, we next traveled to the city's west end and sat through another of those meetings. At that one, there were girls, and more coffee, along with sweet snacks. All of which served to further delay the onset of my hangover."

As I soon learned, each man's commitment to staying sober was deadly serious, and the program meetings were indeed their daily medicine.

"Three girls joined us for dinner after that, at a local restaurant, and then came along to another meeting, this time on the city's north side, after it."

By that time, I had forgotten the hangover, and taken an interest in the company, as well as happenings at the different events.

"I won't deny being distracted by the female company, either."

Much later, Blaine and Steve told me the girls were there to do just that. By doing so, they hoped to distract me, and ease my staying sober.

What can I say? Beyond, it worked.

"So, when midnight rolled around, and the six of us were sharing laughs in a west end coffee shop, the first twenty-four hours were already behind me."

Once again, I was ignorant of a big moment passing.

"I slept late the next day and found a note waiting next to the coffee machine in a kitchen belonging to one of those girls after I got out of the shower. So, I was ready to go when my brother arrived, and we attended a noon meeting together. After it, he went back to work, while I stayed at the club where the meeting took place, because he had already paid for me to have lunch there."

I might have had coffee money in my jeans, but little more. And the need for more of it never came up in those early days, either.

"There was another meeting at two-thirty, and because I was done with lunch, and had nowhere else to be, I took a seat and listened. When it ended, I walked upstairs to find my brother's roommate had showed up, and he asked me to join him for an early dinner."

At the time, I didn't even know what a newcomer was.

But no matter what was happening, either one or the other of my new roommates made a point of footing every bill. In my head, there was a tab running. As the weeks passed, the size of it made me increasingly nervous.

"The two men kept me busy, like that, with at least a couple of meetings a day, and sometimes three or four. And the shakes left my hands, and my belly, after less than a week. By then, I was keeping steady company with one of the girls met the night I arrived. And almost before I knew it, the first two weeks without a drink passed."

I remember being too busy trying to keep up with my new roommates, who rarely, if ever, went without a cup of coffee, to notice. Neither did either of them ever ask me to pay any rent, though I lived, much of the time, in their apartment's spare bedroom.

"But don't get the wrong idea. Because the urge was strong, and no matter how many of the program groups I saw, or how many meetings I went to, in those early weeks, it wasn't doing a thing for me. I stayed dry only because I was broke, not because I was getting sober."

Lucky for me, I'm a big coffee fan, and was soon enough hooked on the stuff. Though I can't remember ever paying for any of it.

"That 'fake it til you make it' crap wasn't working too well, either, and I had no time for the gee-oh-dee thing, let me tell you. In fact, in those days, I had little time for anything but self-will, and none for stuff like logic, faith, gratitude, or common sense!"

I recall thinking myself tossed by the winds of a cruel fate as the days lengthened, the longer I went without a drink. This, despite the soft comfort and near-constant care being lavished upon me at the time. For which I never received a bill.

"Then came a sunny weekday afternoon, when I had been hanging around there, staying dry, for a month or so, and my big brother was driving me home after we had attended another program meeting together. We traveled through midday traffic in downtown Edmonton, as I remember it now. And I decided to tell him that I wasn't getting it, and how it seemed like the world was blowing me around like a ragdoll, and that not drinking wasn't making any of it stop, and how I felt like there was nothing to hold on to, and that nothing in the world was real."

To this day, I'm suspicious of sense data.

"He listened, patient, while piloting the car through the twists and turns of Jasper Avenue, turning into Stony Plain Road, as I spilled my guts. And so, when he signaled to turn right a few blocks later, and then parked, I didn't know what was up. But when he turned off the car's engine, he motioned for me to follow him, and I did."

Only a few yards away, cars streamed by, non-stop.

"For a minute, I thought he was joking when he told me what I was to do next."

I remember hoping he was.

"Because when we got to the corner, my brother walked only a few steps before turning, and pointing to a young fir tree next to him on the boulevard. He then told me to hug it."

I nodded, smiling, as a ripple of laughter passed through the unseen crowd.

"Of course, like anyone with a lick of sense, at first, I refused. But he insisted. Not only that, but he also told me that if I wanted to find out if anything in the world was real, all I had to do was hug that damned tree."

I remember the flush of embarrassment as cars filled with strangers drove past, ignorant of my dilemma.

"By then, though getting sober looked like the only career move left, even staying dry was driving me crazy. And lucky for me, spending much of my young life in a boxing ring got me used to putting up with misery to get what I wanted. Because just then, more than anything else, I wanted to get my career back."

In those days, I remember starting to believe giving up the booze might help me get what I thought it was I wanted.

"So, in afternoon traffic, on one of west Edmonton's busiest streets, I walked over and put a bear hug on that tree, with my big brother egging me on."

In a second, for maybe the first time, I knew what it meant to be vulnerable.

"I still haven't forgotten how my cheeks got hot when a few cars honked their horns as they passed."

I recall hoping no one recognized me standing there. And then, as the world kept moving around me, and the tree remained still, I remember wondering if Steve ever had to do such nonsense to get sober.

*

"Well, that was it," I said, "for me, you know?"

Later that night, I read from the book.

"That night, after getting home, I got busy reading the book. I read it every day, for a while there. I went deep, too, eh? There was no fooling around, either. Because, at last, I got serious about getting sober."

By then, I must have wanted something other than what I had. Though I didn't know what it might be.

"Only a few weeks later, me and my new sponsor were sharing an apartment. Because the same day I met him at the downtown club, I asked that straight-talking construction worker to sponsor me."

I was relieved when he agreed.

"And since then, I've sure been grateful to have one."

Though I didn't know what a program sponsor was supposed to do for me, then.

"Because, while surely no therapist, for me, anyway, my program sponsor remains a resource relied upon for more than advice about living sober."

For me, my program sponsor is one of the most important people in my life.

"To call my sponsor a friend and confidant doesn't even come close to summing it up."

My sponsor is that, and more, to me.

"Not only that, but since reading from that book the first time, I've also had no desire to drink booze."

To me, it was uncanny.

"Anyway, after that night in the restaurant, I started taking the program real serious. And with support from my sponsor, and my home group, which he made me get, by the way, I had worked my way through the steps when my second birthday came around."

While applause passed through the crowd, a thought crossed my mind. When it ended, I shared it.

"And to this day, the thing I'm most grateful for in my life is getting sober."

To me, relief is the greatest gift a sick person can get.

"But you know what they say about a sober horse thief, eh? And how getting dry doesn't mean you're gonna stay that way? Well, I had a hard time with that one, because I didn't want to drink, and never stole anything in my life, either, you know?"

For a while, the metaphor went over my head.

"And like I told you earlier, the charm thing was my go-to move. So, when I was told working with drunks was something that had to be done if I wanted to stay sober, I jumped in with both feet, you know."

I was driving a cab by then, mostly at night, and not enjoying it.

"The trouble was, there were all kinds of girls in the

program, too, and it sure seemed like a lot of them needed my help, you know? And I was just the guy to give it to them, eh? Yup, and right away, too, you know."

The night work left me with lots of time to make step thirteen calls.

"For a while, my friends in the program let me slide on the thirteen-stepping, but it wasn't long before my roomie-slash-sponsor let me know the cat was out of the bag, eh? From then on, I would see the heads turn when I got to a meeting, and lemme tell you, that was no fun."

While uncomfortable, the disapproval wasn't enough to make me stop.

"Because as far as I knew, getting sober didn't come with a morality clause."

For that, I'm grateful.

"And maybe because I blamed the thirteen-step calls on working nights, and driving a hack, my sponsor-slash-roomie, well aware of my struggles, decided to see if he could get me out from behind the wheel? Now, because I didn't ask him about it then, you know, even today, I'm not sure what he was thinking, eh?"

It's another mystery for which I'm grateful to the man upstairs.

"But when I was a little more than two years sober, my sponsor-slash-roomie got me a job at a treatment center, you know? Where the guy running the place was his sponsor. I started part-time on weekends, helping out the counselors as a kind of glorified gopher, wearing a set of hospital whites, eh? And I didn't know it, but they hired me to replace a guy who had returned to drinking."

I must have been ready for a change. My sponsor's raving to me didn't hurt either, as he worked at the place a few years earlier. So, without giving it too much thought, I gave it a whirl.

"See, there's really no better network to be part of than this program and its members, my friends. Not on this earth, anyway, and that's for sure, eh?"

Later, my sponsor told me he thought I was a good fit for the job of helping others get sober.

"Anyway, after landing the job, there was some professional training I had to take for it, too, you know?"

That first return to the classroom opened my eyes.

"Not only that, but right away there was something I liked about the work. Though at first, I didn't know what it was, eh?"

Nowadays, I'm sure it was the experience of working closely with people for a first time.

"So, with the approval of my new boss and support from my sponsor-slash-roommate, I started taking college courses, you know."

Despite the middling grades earned in high school, classroom learning has always come easy for me.

"Less than two years of part time work later, after a year of studying days, and working nights in the cab, I got myself certified as a Life Skills Coach, eh?"

For me, it was a big deal, too.

"I hope I never forget the pride achieving that certification gave me, you know? Nor the thrill of having the book's promises start coming true in my own life."

By then, it had been years since I had accomplished an independent goal.

"So, when a full-time entry level counselor job opened at another area treatment center, with the help of references from my sponsor and my boss, I landed it."

The day I started working there was the same one on which I walked away from the car business for the last time.

"Those early days of counseling work were some of the most fun and fulfilling times of my life, too, eh?"

As usual, for me, charm affected how long I stayed with it.

"But you know, there was a sober horse thief along for the ride, and though I did my best to keep him in check, temptation eventually got the better of me."

With me, progress was slow.

"Anyway, three months into my new job, I qualified for a

one-week-a-month training program in Calgary on the company dime. It stretched over six months for a class of about twenty counselors from across Alberta. On the first day there, they paired the students into training teams. And there I met a girl who would help me take another important step in my sobriety."

I paused for a sip of water and waited for the old hurt to pass before speaking.

"Now, like I told you before, the charm thing is one of my gifts, or so I've been told, anyway, eh?"

The evidence speaks well enough for itself.

"And I was newly sober, and excited to share the gift of it with whoever I could, in those days, too, you know?"

Though I'm not claiming innocence. Neither at home nor abroad.

"So, when the instructor paired me up with this girl, in the classroom, who was in her twenties, and good looking, and fit, and sexy, and smart, well, you know where my head was at, and right away, too, eh?"

She lived in Calgary and worked at a treatment center southwest of the city.

"She, however, had other ideas, and though we got along pretty well, too, you know, there was no hanky-panky. Not that first week, anyway."

I nodded at the memory.

"Not only that, but each of us was still fairly new to sobriety, you know, and right into the work, too, eh? So, while it wasn't easy to keep my lust in check, we made a good team, and I'm pretty sure both of us enjoyed that first week of our working together."

When we parted, I remember looking forward to seeing her the next month.

"But by the middle of the second week of classes the following month, we had gotten to know each other a little better, and there were plenty of sparks flying around, too, you know. So, when I asked her out to dinner on Thursday night, she said yes. The next day, when classes ended, she asked me if

I wanted to stay the weekend. Of course, like any self-respecting bachelor of the time, I agreed."

I paused again and waited for the memories of that first awkward weekend together to pass before getting back to my story.

SEVEN

"See, it was my first time trying the long-distance romance thing, and I had no idea how much work it took."

It was a first stab at love since splitting with my high school sweetie, too.

"Because I had been sober for a while, by then, and no longer feared getting involved with someone, eh?"

I remember being comfortable, and thinking I was in a good place.

"Also, thanks to completing the steps, I no longer had that constant daily fear of getting drunk, you know? In fact, unless I was working with a newcomer, I hardly ever thought about booze in those days."

The obsession to drink, for me, was gone.

"I think I was pretty sure I had things figured out by then, too, eh?"

Life appeared, as I remember it, to be well in hand.

"So, when I started to feel tired, once in a while, after a weekend trip to Calgary and back, I never gave it any thought. Not only that, but me and that girl were going at it hot and heavy before the course ended. Though each of us made it through, and with flying colors, too, you know."

It was a heady time, alright.

"Because I believed myself sober, eh? But later on, I recognized it for what it was. A dry drunk, brought on by complacency and the attitude that comes with it."

Because of which, I soon made a mess of my life.

"And guess what comes with that work-sponsored training, eh? That's right! As soon as you get any kind of certs, the boss expects you to share it with the coworkers. And that ends up adding to your hours on the job, too, doesn't it? Every time!"

Those added working hours, as I look back now, on top of the travel needed for the new romance, wore on me.

"The training, though, was an adventure, you know? And I loved the work, then, too. For sure, I did. At the start, anyway."

For me, a man trying to stay sober, there looked to be no better plan than working with other people trying to do the same thing. But I was missing program meetings while chasing extra credit on the job. And though I didn't know it, courting trouble.

"I was happy to put in the extra hours, too, because I was working for the cause, eh? And I was serious about it. Not only that, but sharing my training turned out to be a fun deal, too. And I met people on staff I wouldn't have otherwise, when passing it on, you know."

With an equal number of male and female counselors, the place boasted an example of employment equity rare for the times.

"Of course, along with those meetings came the usual, for me, temptation. Because that's when I got to know several of my female colleagues, eh? And I couldn't help but spend a little charm on a few of them, either."

Maybe it was the long-distance romance that made it alright. Because I sure wasn't raised that way. I've never been sure. But as with many places, the center discouraged employees from getting together. As usual with a rule such as that, breaking it proved easier done than said.

"So, almost before I knew it, the workplace games started up, you know, and I won't tell you it wasn't fun, either, because it was, eh?"

I remember thinking of it as harmless, at first.

"I mean, there's few thrills bigger than forbidden romance, right? And for me, it always seemed like the more, the merrier, with that stuff, you know?"

The way those things do, before I knew it, they progressed.

"Because there I was, sober and healthy, on the pink cloud,

like some big old puppy dog, looking for somebody to scratch his belly, eh."

Through those six months, I remember missing plenty of program meetings, too.

"Anyway, I missed a lot of meetings while training in Calgary. And not long after that, I got into a secret romance with a couple of women from work, one married, and the other single. At the same time."

Even then, I didn't know why I was doing any of it.

"But what's good for the goose is good for the gander, too, eh? At least, that's what my mom would tell me, or something like it, whenever I told her a heartbreak story. And she told me, boy! Too many times, over the years."

I smiled at my mom, who grinned back at me, while the room shared a chuckle.

"And it turned out my girl in Calgary had secrets of her own, eh? That she never shared with me. Not through all the time we were together."

To me, things were good between us. Better than that, even. Or so I had thought.

"So, after a year of thinking things couldn't be better between us, when I left work at lunchtime on a Wednesday in May, to surprise her with a mid-week visit, I was planning to ask her to marry me. Believe it, or not."

To that point, I remained unaware my ego was out of control. And I sure wasn't prepared for what greeted me when I let myself into her apartment a few hours later.

"She had given me a key to her place after we were together for a few months, but I rarely used it. In fact, before that day, she always knew in advance when I was coming down to Calgary to see her, you know?"

It made sense for it to be that way, too. At least, that's what I thought.

"Because I usually stayed the weekend when I drove down there from Edmonton. So, every other time, it made sense to let her know I was on the way before I showed up, eh?"

On that day, I had wanted to surprise her.

"So, when I let myself into her place that day, she didn't expect me. And that's when I found out she had another love in her life, too."

The sound coming from her bedroom was impossible to mistake. And I remember knowing what I expected to see before I opened the door.

"It stunned me, at first, you know? Despite the girls I was messing around with at work up north."

They were, of course, in her bed together when I walked in and made no attempt to get out of it, either.

"Anyway, I guess the irony was lost on me, eh? And like I told you before, I'm no fighter. So, I really had nothing to say, and wanted even less to do, with the young woman I found sharing my girlfriend's bed."

From the room, I might have heard a collective intake of breath. Or maybe I imagined it.

"It was also pretty clear there was no point asking anybody in there if she wanted to marry me, either, eh?"

What I imagined an impotent rage must be, then filled me.

"For maybe a few seconds, I stood there looking at them, but none of us spoke."

I nodded as a collective sigh passed through the crowd. This time, I knew it was real.

"All the same, though, I knew the score."

There was nothing to do but leave. I turned and walked out.

"So, I left."

I remember dropping the apartment key on a coffee table.

"And I bet you can imagine the feelings as I drove north that night, eh?"

Just the usual suspects; anger, shock, disgust, frustration, lust, and loss.

"The typical bruised male ego of a cheating lover, caught in the act, but unwilling to pay the price for it, had me, you know?"

That and plenty more, too.

"All the way to Red Deer, I kept telling myself, over and over, how she had betrayed me."

Until stopping at the city half-way between Calgary and Edmonton, maybe I had myself convinced.

"But when I stopped to gas up, the smell of my macho bull-crap was stronger than the fumes coming off the pump, you know?"

Insight then caught me off guard.

"Maybe the smell of the gas woke me up? I don't know. But all of a sudden, I just knew. In a second, eh? Just like that, too."

With a certainty I had never experienced before, I knew.

"Anyway, I knew it, and right then. That there were things I needed to face about me, if I planned on staying sober, I mean. Because something told me I was about a step away from taking my next drink. And I was desperate to stay sober."

I remember wanting to stay sober more than any other thing I had ever wanted just then.

"So, for the next hour and a half, until getting home and turning in for a couple hours of shuteye before work, I rehearsed breakup speeches, you know?"

Because that's what I planned to do when I got there.

"And I remember the next morning, bone tired from a long night of talking to myself instead of sleeping, how my fear of facing those women was greater than any concern I had about losing my job."

It was an urge I can't explain.

"Because it's not like I wanted to break up with either of them, you know? It just seemed like, after what went down with my girl at Calgary, something I had to do."

I remember feeling there was a weight sitting on my chest. And just then, I was willing to do whatever I had to, to get rid of it.

"Not only that, but I didn't want to lose my job, either, eh? Because it was a good one, and I liked it, too."

Or maybe the fear of getting drunk drove me. I'm still not sure.

"All I knew then was I needed to get honest with myself. And that meant facing the music with the girls at work."

No matter who, or how much, it might hurt.

Just then, I thought of Travis, and the trail of broken hearts marking the travels for which he was, when we first met, best known.

*

"But while standing there hugging that tree," I said, "for at least a few seconds, it seemed like maybe my big brother was right."

Years later, I still recall how the beating of my heart slowed, so long as I held onto that sapling. Maybe it caught me off guard.

"A moment or two later, when he told me to let go, I was in no hurry, and was also surprised to find my eyes were closed, and I was relaxed, and the world no longer seemed to spin out of control."

I recall making the drive home from there in silence. And wondering at what I had experienced on the busy street.

"We drove home without speaking, and for the rest of that day, for me, the desire to get drunk was gone."

Later, I marked it as a turning point. Back then, I didn't believe it that big a deal.

"But sadly, the feeling didn't last, and maybe a week later, the storm in my head was again out of control. After three months without a drink, I was in a bad way, despite going to at least two, and often more, meetings every day."

I remember there was a pressure growing in my head. But it looked, to me, that I was faking it well enough to fool those nearby.

"Work stuff kept my two sober roommates away from home for a weekend just about then, I think. I'm no longer sure what they were up to, but I know it meant I was left at home alone in the apartment. And while they were gone, something happened."

Both had work-related things to do and had to spend a couple of nights away from Edmonton because of it.

"See, there I was, alone in the big city, with a stash of

emergency cash in the house big enough to get me good and loaded. And like I told you, just then it seemed as if I was cracking up."

They sprang their plans on me at the last minute. I remember Blaine gave me a phone number where I could reach him. I recall playing it cool, and not thinking it was worth worrying over, either.

"Now, until then, my reading of the book was limited, and the only thing I knew about the steps was what I had read on a poster at the sober club downtown. Next to one showing the program's twelve traditions, about which I then knew even less."

Which means I was paying attention to other things when I was there, in case you're wondering. But I had sat next to both of them by then, and listened while they were read aloud many times, too. And, as usual, I have no excuse for my recalcitrant ignorance.

"So, it's not like I had given any thought to taking the damned things, or even understood what they were, or how they might help me."

Though aware of many claims made for it, I remained skeptical of the entire program thing, as I recall.

"Instead, I went to the meetings and didn't drink. And told myself I was killing time until I figured out my next move."

As I now recollect, it was getting to be a lengthy wait.

"But that weekend, the program, and the twelve steps, took on a deeper meaning. For me, anyway."

Soon, another big moment passed with me unaware.

"Here's how it went."

I paused for a sip from the water glass before continuing my story.

"I spent my first night at home alone that weekend in the company of a sober girlfriend, who left after making me lunch the next day. From there, I watched a ballgame on TV before going to a meeting with a different sober friend, a fellow who dropped me off at home on Saturday night, a little after nine o'clock."

For me, the fun and games started then.

"I've never been a big TV fan, either, beyond watching sports. Not now, and certainly not then. So, before the clock struck twelve, I was alone, restless, and craving a drink. And I knew where to get one, too. Because there was a lounge only four blocks away, in a strip mall where a hundred-forty-ninth Street met Stony Plain Road. And before I knew it, I was on the sidewalk, heading that way."

I don't remember what put me there.

"A kind of fever seemed to hit me, then. For at least a while, it was like I lost control of body and mind."

It came on without warning.

"Even now, I don't remember getting dressed or leaving the house that night."

Earlier, the local forecast threatened rain.

"But there I was, on the sidewalk."

The warm night air coated my skin, damp but invisible.

"As I recall it now, traffic was light. And the further I walked down Stony Plain Road towards the lights at One-Forty-Ninth Street, the less aware I became of what I was doing. But I remember sweating, and having a knot in my throat, and a pressure in my head, all of it getting worse, the closer I got to the strip mall on the corner."

Something pushed me onward, but I don't know what it was.

"I remember, too, how it felt like something was pushing me."

Maybe it was only the wind at my back.

"Because four blocks passed in a blur, and when I stopped for the traffic lights on the corner, I couldn't even recall stepping out of the apartment door."

The flashing red hand of a traffic signal had jarred me.

"Then, and even now, it's what I imagine sleepwalking must be like."

And I couldn't wake myself.

"I remember being surprised to find myself crossing a parking lot and approaching the entrance to a lounge."

In memory, I floated more than walked.

"Then, from out of that sweaty blur, the words of the first step appeared, like a banner, unfurled across the front page of my mind. And right there, I knew, for the first time, that I was powerless over booze, and managing my life wasn't ever going to be possible for me."

I then arrived at the lounge's entrance door.

"Now, at this point, some folks think I'm either trying to be dramatic, or that I'm even crazier than I look. Others figure I'm just full of it. And, however you choose to hear it, I don't mind. Because all I can share with you is my experience."

At the time, I claimed to be agnostic. But I wanted to believe in something. Because it was essential to getting sober. I had often been told that by then.

"Now, to be clear about it, back then, I told people I was agnostic, whereas, nowadays, I report my status as atheist."

That's a tough one for plenty of folks.

"See, for me, faith is faith, whatever version of it works for you. Because, whether you think there's something, nothing, or you aren't sure about any of it, you believe in it."

For me, that's close enough to the dictionary's definition of faith.

"Anyway, to me, it's important you know that before I tell you the next part."

I paused while a murmur passed through the room.

"Because when I grabbed that lounge door handle, something like a shock hit me and woke me up."

Or so it was for me, then. As if I was coming out of a dream.

"I remember stumbling back, away from the door, and bumping into a couple of fellows on their way into the place. They must have thought I was loaded, because they just laughed at me, and I hurried away."

I recall my hand throbbing as though it were burned. And my head spinning, as if I was drunk.

"A heavy rain must have started, as I retraced my steps to the empty apartment."

By the time I got back there, it had soaked my clothes, and me.

"Though I don't remember getting home too well anymore."

My memories of those few minutes, hazy then, are little more than a mirage now.

"Now, I'm not sure what went on there, but it was most likely some kind of mental or emotional breakdown."

That much, at least, is plain.

"What I know is, when I got back to my brother's home a few minutes later, I was sure about a couple of things."

I'll never forget how I felt after I got out of the shower, either. And though I didn't know it, that was, for me, the dawn of recovery.

"Because I had found out two things about me, I didn't know before taking that walk in the rain. One, I was an alcoholic. And two, I didn't want to drink."

I remember feeling something had changed, but not knowing what it was.

"I didn't know it, but for me, it turned out that accepting my problem was enough to relieve my obsession with the stuff."

Since that long ago night, I've never again wanted to drink booze.

"And today, those same two things are true."

I nodded as the murmur of approval rose from the unseen crowd.

"Because here, now, always, and forever, I'm an alcoholic. And since that night, I've never wanted a drink of booze."

And right there, I thought of Blaine, and how taking the steps was eased by what he had told me years ago.

*

"There was no bigger prize for me," I said, "in those days, than a chance to help my younger brother get sober."

I had been hoping to help get him off the bottle since he took the twenty questions test in my car when I was home on holidays. That was only a couple of years after I got sober myself.

"Because, by then, there was no longer a shred of doubt that my little brother, like me, had a big problem with booze."

Sadly, along with everyone else in the family, I was forced to watch as he took a public fall from grace. Because, when boozing, he focused on ruining his life.

"So, when he showed up asking me to help him learn how to live, I was ready to overwhelm him with the program."

I grinned as the memory of my joy at his arrival returned. Mostly, I was relieved when he hit his personal bottom before killing himself. For many who knew him then, including me, it came as something of a surprise.

"I guess we were both lucky my sponsor reigned me in, too. Because of that, my little brother got to live the program at his own speed."

Which, as I remember it now, was likely too fast for anyone but him.

"Not only that, but I should say he wasn't anybody's little anything, not anymore, by that time. He was a full-grown man. And a whole lot more than anybody wanted to tangle with, too, either in or out of a boxing ring."

Even for me, he could sometimes be scary.

"But that pulling thing was really strong, for me, then. Though I didn't say anything about it to my little brother. Not only that, but I relied on the book whenever he asked for guidance."

I remember having to restrain myself from overwhelming him with program info. And how there was so much I wanted to share with him. But my sponsor made sure I gave him enough space to live it for himself.

"I also relied on my sponsor, for support and direction, maybe more than I had since sobering up myself, then. He made sure it was straight up old school stuff I shared with my little brother, too. Just don't drink, go to meetings, and read the book. With plenty of rest, good food, and sober company, on top of it, like that, at first."

I knew a wish to get back in the ring drove his want to stay sober.

"And because my little brother told me he needed to get back into shape, with help from a buddy in the program, we got him a low-profile spot, at the Indian and Metis Friendship Center gym downtown, where he could train. The benefits of exercise, for him, were plain right away, too. Because he started eating and sleeping better when he got back into it."

His recovery was the focus of many of my off-work hours.

"It also seemed like the longer my little brother stayed sober, the more comfortable I got with that pulling deal happening to me. Because in my life, staying sober was the number one concern then, and remains so to this day."

That's because I'm an alcoholic.

"Though it's more than twenty-five years since my last drink, now, the most important thing for me, every day, is reminding myself that I'm an alcoholic."

It's the only fact I remind myself of each day.

"Because it's alcohol-ism, not alcohol-wasm."

It's a chronic, progressive, and life-threatening illness.

"So, while sharing everything I then knew about the program with my younger brother and devoting as much time as I could to his recovery was the biggest deal going, this is a selfish program. And staying sober was then, and is now, job one for me."

Despite the selfish nature of my program, helping my little brother get sober gave me a needed reminder.

"Anyhow, by then, after seven years, I may have thought I knew it all, or at least, most of everything that mattered, about getting sober. Because my take on the program, as far as I was concerned, was the goods. That's what I believed, from the tip of my longest hair to the soles of my feet, and if you asked me, I'd tell you about it."

Not only that, but staying sober opened all kinds of doors for me.

"I remember how the work seemed to keep pulling me on, too, in those days. And the way I went looking for more training."

For several years, the search for knowledge drove me.

"See, throughout my career, I studied something, somewhere, every year, to improve my professional skills."

Workshops and training often took the place of holidays, too.

"That's mostly because I don't have a degree, from anywhere but the school of hard knocks, and often feel intimidated by my colleagues, because of my lack of a formal education."

Education is another thing I encourage nowadays.

"But to me, all that catch-up schooling also helped me stay sober. Though I only encourage it because I think it improved the quality of my sobriety, too. And that of my life, as well."

To me, it's a selfish program.

"So, my little brother got as much time as there was leftover."

Which was not that much when I look back on it now. My roommate and best friend Steve helped me out plenty, too, in those days. I remember being grateful he was there.

"I did my best not to impose too many of my own beliefs on my younger brother's walk through the early days of recovery. In fact, I was so happy to see him staying dry that I didn't push him too hard about taking the steps, either. Not right away, anyhow."

For me, his staying dry was a good enough start.

"So, you can imagine how thrilled I was when he asked me about taking them, after spending a weekend at home alone. Where I figured, he must have made something of a breakthrough, though he said nothing about it to me."

As my brother progressed, it surprised me to find myself becoming more secure in the terms of my own recovery, and sure of my commitment to the work I was doing.

"Not long after that, on a regular day at work, a few months after my little brother got to Edmonton, when I was counseling someone, who I've long since forgot, I came to believe what I was doing was a calling, and not a choice."

Since then, that's how I've looked at my work.

"It wasn't a big deal either, the way it happened. Since then, though, that's how I look at it."

The truth is, I barely noticed, at the time.

"But on that day, and I've even forgotten what day of the week it was, by now, listening to my patients seemed different. So did sharing my experience, strength, and hope with them."

The change affected everyone, not just me.

"For the first time, I felt myself relax at work. Instead of concern, I felt confidence. Because at last, I was aware of my actions matching my beliefs. I was fearless. Though I was humbled, too, by my new awareness."

My clients knew something had changed, as well.

"To me, it was plain my clients knew something was different, too, and better. Though neither of us knew what it was. Or mentioned it, either."

In the quiet of an unassuming night, my fears had stolen away.

"Not only that, but the same day, I accepted that weird pulling thing as part of my sober journey. From that day, wherever it leads me, I do my best to follow."

Even then, it was leading to more of the knowledge I wanted, and needed, too.

"Because it's more than my job, sharing experience, strength, and hope with you, and people like my little brother and the clients at the center where I then worked. It's also how I express my gratitude for what getting sober gave me."

I hate using a flighty word for a real event, but epiphany might come closest to describing what happened to me that day.

"And just like accepting the pulling thing, this new awareness came without any kind of flash, like in a book or a movie."

But I knew it, and at once, too.

"That day I knew, so long as I did my part, which meant staying sober, going to meetings, reading the book, applying the principles, and showing up for work every day, I could live an authentic life."

Since that day, I've entrusted myself to it.

"Now, near as I can tell, anyhow, my new awareness showed up by itself. All I had to do was accept it. Just like that. And since that day, I've known I was in the right place, and doing the right stuff, and that getting sober was key to the whole thing."

The insight told me this gift was mine. But to keep it, I had to give it away.

"Just like that, the answers I needed to live in a world filled with fear, doubt, and ignorance were clear. All I had to do was stay sober and help others. And if I gave away what I had, more of it would be given to me. In abundance. Somehow, I knew it."

Though I can't say how I came to know.

"Awareness had filled me."

It had caught me off guard, too.

"Though I still don't know how it got there."

In that moment, for the first time, I felt a new faith.

"Or why it came, either."

I'm still grounded by it.

"For me, though it seemed like an entirely real mental and emotional event, what happened that day is what I call a spiritual experience."

I believe that, too. Though I don't blame my little brother for any of it.

"And since having it, my commitment to helping others get sober, and staying that way myself, has remained absolute, and the first concern in my life."

Nowadays, I'm sure I owe everything to that.

EIGHT

"Since that day, for me, there's been no doubt."

That's a fact.

"But when the job offer came, it meant a move back to Calgary, the scene of many earlier crimes as I told you before, and let me tell you, that was a little scary."

I owed amends to my ex and wasn't looking forward to making them.

"So, it took a while to make up my mind about going back down there."

When my brother turned up, I had lived at Edmonton for ten years and been sober through the last seven of them.

"Because life, for me, was good at Edmonton. The work was steady, as a home-school liaison with an inner-city school, where I was given plenty of training. After five years at the same job, a steady paycheck had me living in style. And with a sponsee as my roommate, there was little pressure from girlfriends to get serious."

I stuck to a simple code of program focused living.

"Not only that, but in those days, program service work took up most of my spare time. And to this day, I encourage newcomers to get involved doing it. Because nothing helps a person stay sober more than helping someone else get that way. That's a fact, my friends, you can take it to the bank."

I paused as a murmur of reply passed through the room.

"Anyhow, like I told you, after my kid brother showed up, keeping him on the path to sobriety was holding the number one spot on my to-do list. So, when a chance to spend a summer in the mountains with him, my roomie, and a legendary Indigenous Medicine Man came along, I jumped at it."

The school where I then worked held a series of summer camps for students at a First Nation between Calgary and Banff. With another boom in the patch underway that year, royalties paid to the province by Big Oil were footing the bill. Instead of the usual ragged quilt of program funding and charitable donations.

"See, our school needed youth counselors for the annual summer camp held on a First Nation west of Calgary. So, I hired my younger brother, then only three or four months sober, and my newly unemployed but years-sober roommate. And to say I got pushback from my boss about my choices would be an understatement."

I remember being not nearly so confident in them as I claimed to be.

"With few prospects at the time, selling my little brother on the plan was easy enough."

Though not convinced he could pull it off, I knew he needed the money.

"While for my roomie, who was a certified life coach and experienced addictions counselor, by then, it would be a summer to cool off after losing his treatment center job. Besides, he had rent to pay."

Both of us had learned that life went on, too, despite either plans or circumstances, even in sobriety.

"Not only that, but hiring the well-trained roomie made getting my greenhorn little brother taken on easier. I remember selling them to my boss as some kind of package deal."

Lucky for us, I've always been a good salesman.

"Anyhow, by then, one thing seemed clear enough to me. And that's this: for people trying to get or stay sober, and most others, too, earning a living has a profound and positive effect on the self-esteem."

I'm sure of that, too.

"So, when the first of the two-week camp outs began, there was more than enough excitement to go around."

The school ran four of the two-week long camping trips for

students between the end of June and late August. For me, and many of my colleagues, it was both a reward and the highlight of a school year spent working with them and their families.

"And maybe it was the mountains, or it could have been the kids, I'm not sure, but that summer helped make up my mind. About a lot of stuff, too."

I didn't even know much of it had been on my mind.

"What I know is, when I got there, I thought one way about some things, and when I left, I believed different, about a few of them, at least."

Nowadays, when I remember what happened to me up there, I accept it as another spiritual experience.

"See, at each camp, we rode shotgun over two dozen kids, who amounted to a multicultural gang of students from thirteen to seventeen years old."

With help from venue staff, we had adults keeping an eye on them day and night.

"Equal numbers of girls and boys attended, and we had a staff of twelve, with five female counselors, the same number of men, plus myself and my boss, who was also a woman."

Each of us worked closely with the kids, too.

"So, with another couple of dozen local staff around, plus our counselors and their security staff at night, the safety of the young campers was pretty much guaranteed. I can't say the same for the rest of us."

Aside from myself and Travis, none of the counselors were too familiar with the wilderness.

"But, aside from needing a mountainside rescue, for a couple of over-zealous kids, and what seemed daily cases of poisoned oak, our weeks out there were plenty of fun, despite long days of pretty hard work."

The kids were busy from sunup until past dark, seven days a week.

"When we got there, they put all of us, counselors and kids, to work right away, too."

We helped the venue staff raise eight teepees, and there we

slept, outside, beside a lake next to the First Nation owned resort hosting our group.

"But every morning, they served a huge breakfast to everyone in the dining room of the big lodge up there."

It was an impressive place.

"The lodge was made of massive, fitted logs, and along with its outbuildings, was both rugged and gorgeous. I know every time we went up there, everyone, from kids to counselors, was amazed by the natural beauty of that place."

We kept the kids busy while they were there, too.

"Anyhow, every day, after a big breakfast, nature walks, canoeing, sports, and cultural awareness filled the hours between then and lunchtime."

Everyone burned plenty of calories up there.

"Then, another huge meal was served to our group at noon, again in the lodge's beautiful dining room overlooking the lake."

The place was a dream come true.

"Followed by even more activities, all outdoors, weather permitting."

I remember the food was both plentiful and delicious.

"After a big dinner in the lodge, stuff like campfires, astronomy, music, and stories kept the young campers busy until snack-time. Though of course, rounding them up and getting them into bed soon got to be a nightly game nobody, aside from the kids, enjoyed."

I hosted an informal program meeting on Wednesday nights in the lodge, after the lights went out for the students.

"But the place was peaceful, too, and everyone enjoyed being there. And right from the first week, the three of us, my roomie, my little brother, and me, started getting together on Wednesday nights in the lodge for an informal program meeting. As the summer went along, getting sober, and staying that way, kind of went hand in hand with the whole deal we were working on with those kids up there."

It was plain, to me anyhow, that a shared concern for those kids gave each of us a focus far beyond the everyday.

"Just like caring for those kids meant all of us had to keep our eyes on something other than ourselves. Every day, too. So, for all of us working there, it was a summer spent living with the stress of being responsible for something."

To me, it was more of the direct service work I believe is so important to recovery. But I watched both of my roommates, real close, for signs of trouble, just the same.

"Lucky for me, as I hoped, the service work helped my little brother get sober, while for my roomie and myself, it reminded us of why we wanted to stay that way."

I know fresh air does a body good, too.

"Anyhow, that summer, after surviving night one at the place, the next morning we met the Medicine Man. He would be with us on most days when we were at the resort. And under his guidance, on the first day, we helped build what's called a sweat lodge. Now, I can't talk too much about cultural matters, only about stuff for which I've got permission. Because just like anonymity is a big deal to us here, so too is respect for our culture to my people. Hai, hai."

I nodded to the grandfathers before sipping from the water glass.

"The Medicine Man showed us what to do. And how to get it done, too. But we, the kids, and the counselors, built the sweat lodge. With everyone helping, it took only an afternoon. We made it out of small saplings, and larger willows, mostly. With not a hammer or a nail to be found, either."

I paused a moment and remembered how building the ingenious dome-shaped design had astounded me.

"The Medicine Man picked and cut the trees and willows used to build it, using only a hatchet. He then showed us where to bend and tie and place the pieces he cut. All by hand, with every bit made by us and the first group of kids."

Even now, I recall how the kids surprised me the first day.

"But what I remember most is how those kids just listened to that Old Man. To them, he seemed way beyond us, the counselors, and maybe even above their parents. And right away, too. Whenever they were with him, no matter what they were doing, he seemed to hold them spellbound."

The Old Man didn't appear to notice.

"Right from the start, whenever he talked about anything, his authority went unquestioned, by either them or us."

For me, he, too, was something out of a dream.

"Later groups of kids would get to hang out with the Medicine Man, too, and haul wood, or talk with him, before the ceremonies."

The Old Man, though spry enough, was then known to be in his eighties.

"But all the time we were there, with all the kids who came to see him, and us, too, the effect he had on everyone was the same."

I remember how the Medicine Man was not only unaware of the impact he had upon the group, but unaffected by it.

"I remember thinking, then, about how natural it all seemed. Despite being so out of character for those kids. Or for me, and our counselors, too, for that matter."

Most times, dealing with our group was more like herding cats than anything else.

"The kids would also help my roomie-slash-counselor heat the rocks he placed at the center of the sweat lodge's dome-like structure before the start of the ceremonies. Sometimes they helped him rearrange the hides that formed its roof, too."

Without a word spoken, Steve was appointed as the Old Man's helper. He made no complaint over that, either. At least, not to me. I remember thinking he must have liked it. That's how it looked, anyhow.

"Through that summer, every week, a different group of the student campers, under my roomie-slash-counselor's guidance, would cut and carry wood, and then build and maintain the fire needed to heat the rocks used inside the lodge."

I remember Steve got tight with the Old Man soon after we arrived.

"Before too long, the place had an atmosphere. Not only that, but my roomie-slash-counselor and the Old Man struck up a friendship right away, too."

The sweat lodge was a mile or so northwest of the resort, in a clearing on the south side of a Rocky Mountain foothill, just below the place where the tree line gives way to the slope.

"It was a fair hike away from the resort and into the foothills, too, of at least a mile, for the kids to get to the sweat lodge. And the Old Man would spend at least an hour with them, while they rested after getting there, sharing the culture. He would always thank them before they started and again when they finished their work, too, before going into the lodge for a ceremony."

Inside, there was room for the Old Man and three or four others to sit around steaming hot rocks placed in a hole in the middle of the sweating hide walls of the pitch-dark lodge.

"In there, at least a few afternoons a week, the Old Man talked with the spirits. When the weather allowed, he invited any of the adults in our party who wished to join him, in small groups, for the cultural ceremony. But though allowed to help prepare and maintain the sweat lodge, the kids weren't allowed to take part in them."

With approval from my boss, who attended many of the sweats, I encouraged the counselors to try it. Over the summer, most of them did, at least once.

"As field leader of our counselor group, and Indigenous, it made sense for me to show them the way. So, I was ready for the first one. The Old Man told us what to do, and I remember going into the lodge with great respect, and what I presumed was an open mind."

When the ceremony was over, I was no longer sure it was open.

"Now, before going on, it's worth knowing that I believe getting sober required me to make a spiritual journey. I also believe staying that way means I need to have a personal relationship with a higher power of my own understanding. I believed this then, as I still do today."

In those days, that pulling thing, which by then I'd accepted as, at least somewhat, normal, for me, was leading me closer to my Indigenous roots. Meeting the Old Man brought it into sharper focus.

"So, even by then, respect for the beliefs of others was already strong in me, because I was getting to know a little more about a lot of things. Or maybe helping others get sober was changing my mind about what I thought it was I believed."

Truth is, I wasn't sure then and doubt I ever will be.

"All I know is the Medicine Man got to me. I don't know when, either, because I didn't spend that much time with him. But he sure got into my head. Or maybe it was my heart."

I don't even remember it happening.

"Anyhow, he must have. Because there's no other answer, beyond the spiritual, that says I'm not crazy for telling you what happened to me in there, and that's a fact."

I paused again, as memory sped my heart and made me want for a deeper breath.

"And just in case anyone is worried, don't be. Because I asked the Old Man for permission to share this part of my story long ago."

As far as I'm concerned, anonymity is the most important of our program's principles. Since learning it, I've done my best to extend that same respect to everyone, no matter their walk of life.

"Before going into the sweat lodge, that first time, the Old Man told us if anyone wanted to ask him a question, he would request an answer to it, from the grandfathers, during the ceremony."

I remember being surprised, and curious, too.

"Later, I told myself I did what I did next out of respect for the process, and to lead my fellow counselors into the waters, so to speak. But at the time, what he said caught me off guard."

Maybe I reacted to his suggestion without thinking.

"So, I asked him a question about my late father. Though, of course, I expected nothing to come of it."

When we entered the sweat lodge, I remember a great

respect for my parent's culture filling my heart.

"Like I told you before, there's a limit on what I can say about it, but it was the most powerful thing of that kind I've ever known. And I wasn't ready for stuff that strong yet, though I didn't know it."

In the sweat lodge, I was convinced my father spoke to me.

"But, when it was over, and I came out of that animal hide-covered dome, the world, and me, too, seemed to have changed."

I started a different journey on that day.

But just then, I thought of my brother Travis, and the challenges he faced while locked away with us there at that mountain camp.

*

"Not long after that," I said, "my big brother got me a job, working as a camp counselor with inner-city kids, believe it or not, in the foothills west of Calgary. By then, though I wasn't ready to get back into a boxing ring, I was near desperate to make myself a dollar. So, despite not having a clue about doing that kind of work, I jumped at the chance, and was grateful to get it, too. As he would be there, and his roommate as well, it also sounded like more of a holiday than it turned out to be."

Lucky for me, the wages were generous.

"So, when the first of those two-week summer camps started, there was plenty of goodwill happening at my end. But at the same time, I was also trying to take the steps, and having a hell of a time with it."

Don't get the wrong idea, as I've only been a skeptic since childhood.

"Anyway, let's just say I was asking my big brother a lot of questions in those days, and most of them were about the steps and how to take them."

While plain enough now, I didn't yet know how much I liked to complicate most things then.

"To say many of his answers didn't please me would also be an understatement, and that's for sure. Because he was kind of sickening with his replies to most of them. At least, I remember thinking he was. And, not getting what it was he was trying to show me drove me crazy, too. Or, at least, that's what I claimed."

In fact, I was afraid.

"Because really, it scared me. I mean, what might happen to me if I took more of those steps?"

I paused a beat before again speaking.

"Would it mean I might have to stay sober forever?"

As a ripple of laughter filled the room, I sipped from the water glass. When the laughs ended, I continued my story.

"See, I still wasn't sure what it meant to be sick like I was. Or how doing things like taking the steps could possibly help me."

I did not yet understand either my illness or myself.

"And my brother and his roommate, too, stuck to the same story, no matter how many times I tried to get them to change it to suit me."

To them, it was a simple deal.

"But when those summer camps started, though I was thinking it might be ok for me to be powerless over the booze, that was mostly because I still had a manager, somewhere, waiting for me to get it together. Somehow, that seemed to give me an out for giving up self-control, maybe. At least, in my mind, I think it did."

Though I couldn't make it without the help of a manager, the idea of any power greater than me then was, frankly, offensive. For a fighting man, it was asking too much.

"As a skeptic, meanwhile, though I looked at people with either spiritual or religious beliefs with something less than hatred, in those days, there was little more than pity reserved for such weaklings, as I recollect it now."

I still believe in the scientific method. Though today I'm more accepting of its limits.

"But my big brother was patient with me, and I'm sure grateful to him for that. He was also quite rigid, though, and I'll always be thankful for that, too. Because no matter what I tried, he always gave me the same answers."

Even when I got pissed at him for repeating them.

"He gave it to me by the book and never wavered."

Because that's how it works.

"So, his typical response to a question about step two, would be something like, take God out of it, and substitute whatever works as a source of strength greater than yourself, even if it's the group or its people, or the Sun, or Einstein, or something like that. Whatever. It makes no difference. Not to you getting sober, he would tell me. What's important is accepting the idea of something with knowledge or strength beyond your own."

Then, a usual finishing line.

"Fake it 'til you make it, eh, kid? he would say, then, he'd look at me and go, Kapeesh?"

To this day, aside from his gangster talk, I don't know what made such a simple thing so hard for me to understand.

"Even so, the struggle for acceptance, for me, was real, and every day, too. I tried praying, and sought guidance from the book, though it didn't occur to me that bouncing around from one topic to another, instead of reading it front-to-back, made little sense. Much as my reading of the steps ignored the natural order of their sequence, as I searched in vain for an easier, softer way."

Though now years sober, I still prefer having things my own way. It's a defect, and I know it. But I seek progress, not perfection.

"My favorite of his answers was what he told me when I asked him how to go about taking the steps. And I was serious, too, when I asked, because I wanted to restore my old life, and staying off the booze looked like the only way to do it, right then."

In those days, I was sure getting my career back was the most important thing getting sober could give me.

"So, when he asked me if I knew how to count, you can guess the kind of reply he got."

I remember him laughing at my response.

"Then he told me if that were true, the answer was staring me in the face."

Again, aside from alcoholism, I have no answer for why it was so hard for me to see how simple things are, way back when.

"Then he asked me to count to twelve, aloud, so he could hear me, to prove it."

Too surprised by the ask to do otherwise, I started counting.

"After letting me count to a dozen, he held up a hand to stop me, and nodded, and then says, there you go my bud, just like that, that's how you do the steps, same way, one after the other, in order, just the way you counted to twelve there."

I remember being choked at him for blowing me off that way.

"And it angered me, at first. But when it turned out he was sincere, it scared me. Even more than my earlier ignorance."

I remember how hard it still was for me to think clearly then.

"Then, after taking a minute to think about what he said, from within the cavernous dark of my tortured melon, the dawn of insight, like a plastic lighter held aloft at a rock concert, alone in the pitch-dark of my closed mind, barely flickered."

I recall it seeming too good to be true.

"One after the other, from one to twelve, in order, just like that, is how I would take the steps. Just as they were written. Exactly as they're counted. The same way any set of steps, no matter where you find them, either real or metaphorical, must be climbed."

I got it.

"Just like that, I had it. But when the power of that simple idea hit me, it went off inside my head like I'd been cracked by an unseen left hook."

For which, by the way, I've long been a sucker.

"And for a minute there, I remember wondering if what I felt was what people meant when they claimed their minds were blown."

I recall feeling a need to lock my core and plant my feet.

"Still, I would spend much of those weeks in the mountains struggling to make it up the first three steps. And on many days, it felt like they were going to be too much for me."

Though I had no want to drink, the idea I might, or could,

scared me, too.

"But my brother held a meeting for the three of us every Wednesday night in the lodge, after the kids were in bed, and it proved a lifeline for me."

It turns out program meetings truly are medicine for sick people.

"Not only that, but those two men, my brother, and his roommate, held my hand as I fought my demons and tried to get sober out there."

Without them, I'm sure this story ends long ago, for me.

"For that, I'll never be too grateful. Because as far as I'm concerned, I owe them my life. And friends, it's been a good one."

It sure has.

But just then, I thought of our old roommate Steve, and how he helped me stick with it out there, despite troubles of his own.

*

"So, when my roommate, who like I told you before was also my sponsor," I said, "offered me a couple of months work at a summer camp in the mountains west of Calgary, riding herd on a bunch of school kids, I was in a mood for getting away, and took him up on it, you know."

When I lost my job, a few weeks before he offered me the camp thing, there was no severance package.

"Though, after losing my treatment center job for fraternizing, the state of my savings meant I wasn't in a place to be too picky, either, eh? But knowing my roomie and his brother would be up there with me, it sounded like fun, too. The money was also decent, and though I've said nothing about it, I've always liked kids, you know."

I nodded in reply to the murmur that passed through the crowd seated in front of me.

"Besides, I was hurting pretty good, and maybe I figured getting back to nature would help me get closer to the man upstairs, or something, eh? I don't know. But it turned out to be a great fit, and right away, too, for me."

The lodge hosting the summer camps featured an

impressive two-story main building made of oversized, and sometimes intricately carved, logs. It was set well back from the highway and surrounded by a complex of smaller log structures made in the same style.

"The lodge hosting the camps was on a First Nation about forty-five minutes west of Calgary. It stood on the north side of a small lake in the foothills of the Rocky Mountains and remains one of the most beautiful places I've ever seen, you know."

On arrival, and struggling with still recent heartbreak, I recall being overpowered by what first looked a too-close shave with nature.

"Now, remember I was struggling with a minor case of the old broken heart when we got there, eh?"

The place looked to be something out of a dream.

"And, let me tell you, that place was beautiful. When we got there, it almost brought tears to my eyes. But having to look out for a bunch of unruly city kids sure pulled me out of that, and quick, you know?"

It didn't take them five minutes to remind me I was there to work.

"I've also been a camera buff since junior high school, you know, and I brought a couple of them up there with me, and lots of film, too, eh?"

The camera was again a steady companion by then.

"Almost as soon as we got there, if I remember it right, we helped the staff set up several authentic Indigenous teepees next to a small lake in front of the lodge, too."

They were to be our home for the summer.

"I remember snapping shots of the kids and the counselors helping the venue staff get those teepees built."

Before the summer ended, I took pictures of most everything we did. Along with everyone who took part.

"By then, I had converted the closet in my Edmonton bedroom into a darkroom, eh? And I must have been taking pictures again for at least a year already."

A schoolboy's hobby, long lost, had returned to my life.

"See, taking pictures was a hobby I picked up in junior high. But gave up when drinking and work took more of my time."

After getting sober and returning to steady work, the first thing I bought for myself was a camera.

"It's funny how getting sober showed me what I really missed, you know? That's how it seemed to me, anyway, eh? Like I had forgotten who I was, and what I enjoyed, and maybe what I wanted, too, while I'd been so busy drinking."

My first years of living sober were a getting to know me period, where I found a new, but old, me.

"And it turned out the teepees were our homes for the summer. I still remember how the first night in a sleeping bag on the ground left me groggy the next day, too, like someone had poured sand into my head while I slept."

After a cup of hot coffee in the lodge, I felt better.

"I had a little trouble with my balance that first week out there, but remember chalking it up to the altitude, and fresh air, and excitement. Not only that, but the kids had far more energy than I was ready for, and the other counselors were pretty much wasted at the end of the days, too, you know? So, again, I didn't give it much thought."

There was enough going on with those kids every day to leave little time for the selfish concerns of anyone on staff. In that environment, I remember it was easy enough to ignore mine.

"Besides, the next day, we met the Medicine Man. After that, the whole deal turned into a journey unlike any I'd taken before it. Or since, my friends."

Even today, I'm not sure which parts of it were real, and what I might have imagined.

"We met the old man the day after our group arrived. And somehow, I got assigned to lead the first group of kids charged with helping him build a cultural sweat lodge."

Beyond a sweet disposition and an ever-present smile, the Old Man oozed a calm that spread to those nearby. He showed us what to do, and then watched, or helped, but spoke little the first day.

"Now, before I go on, it's important to remember I was raised in a Christian home. And at that time, was trying to build a closer, and personal, relationship with my higher power, as I understood it."

By then, my sponsor was getting into his Indigenous culture, and maybe I was looking around, hoping to find direction, or something, eh? I'm not sure.

"So, along with the recent heartbreak, it seems I was either open-minded or hurt bad enough to pay attention when the man upstairs gave me a sign, you know."

That's how I see it, nowadays.

"Because the steps changed my life and left me wanting more of what I tapped into after turning my life over to what I then thought of as the, not my, higher power."

I was looking for something.

"The freedom to choose, and to seek, wasn't what I expected getting sober to be about, either, you know?"

At first, the idea of so much freedom scared me.

"But no matter where I went, to different cities, at roundups, meetings, or anywhere sober program folks got together, open minds seemed to be everywhere. And along with them came different ways of learning, thinking about, and living sober. For a newcomer like me, it was almost too much to handle at first, you know? My sponsor told me to keep it simple, and to that point, I guess I did."

The program, and stuff related to it, filled my calendar through those first couple of years after getting sober.

"But like I told you before, I was raised to believe a certain thing. And maybe I supposed I always would, too, eh?"

Just then, it was as though what I claimed to believe no longer felt comfortable.

"So, out there, when the Medicine Man told us we could ask him questions, and he would ask what he called the grandfathers, for answers on our behalf, I was kind of surprised to find I had a list in my head, ready for him, you know?"

Though we had by then lived together for several years, it scared me to ask Blaine for details related to his Indigenous culture. Despite getting more curious, the longer we lived as roomies.

"I signed up for the first ceremony the Medicine Man held in that sweat lodge we built and went to them as often as I could for as long as we were there after that, too, eh? Over the summer, I must have been in there ten or maybe even fifteen times."

As the summer went on, my health flagged, and an hour sweating in the darkness relieved a clogged feeling in my chest. I remember having many questions for the Old Man, too.

"But I didn't ask the Medicine Man any questions in the sweat lodge until the last few weeks of our time with him, you know, because I wasn't sure if I was being honest or just curious. And when I asked my sponsor-slash-roomie about it, he told me I would know the answer when the time was right. I also remember being pissed at him for that, you know?"

I nodded to the crowd as a ripple of laughter passed through the room.

"Because that summer opened my eyes to some stuff. The Medicine Man and I ended up spending a lot of time together. We talked about all kinds of things, too. And I felt some kind of weird bond with him, you know, after building the sweat lodge. I mean, I'm not even sure if he had any idea about it. But he treated me nice, anyway, and when I asked him for help with my next career move, it seemed like both of us were sincere, eh?"

As the summer's end neared, I found myself with little want to go back to working in a treatment center.

"Now don't get me wrong, because I loved the camp counselor thing, and if that were a full-time job, even up there, I might have just stayed with it, you know. But when summer ended, the ride would be over, and I would have to find some work. Or file a claim for unemployment insurance, which I feared, eh?"

The prospect of having too much free time on my hands still scared me then.

"Anyway, respect for the culture keeps me from getting too specific about it. But after a summer of sharing with the Medicine Man, I knew it was time for me to leave Alberta. And I was ready to follow my heart."

Because taking the steps meant getting sober. In turn, that meant I could now chase my dreams without fear of either failure or regret. More important? I no longer had any interest in drinking.

"The Medicine Man told me I was free, and that it wasn't an illusion. All I had to do was stay on my path, and the grandfathers would always be with me."

As it told me in the book, what I had to do was don't drink, go to meetings, and read it.

NINE

"So, when we got back to Edmonton, I decided it was time to make a move, and return to school, as well, you know?"

Despite losing his roommate, my sponsor supported the plan.

"Only a few months later, with nearly four years of sobriety, I went ahead and moved back out to Vancouver Island. Not only that, but almost as soon as I got there, I enrolled myself in college."

I returned to classes in the fall and spent the next two years in school.

"And the miserable cold of winter on the prairies had nothing to do with me leaving, my friends. But I sure don't miss it, eh?"

A chuckle passed through the room. And I remember being surprised to find getting sober made school, for me, something of a treat.

"Mostly, it was really nice being close to my folks again, and not just because they're both sober, either."

I was lonely for family now and then while living on the prairies.

"Because with no family living in Alberta, I had missed my folks, and my sister, too."

After figuring that out, sobriety meant I could change it.

"Don't forget, my dad, my sister, and my uncle are all in the program, too, you know. And you remember where they send those people who can't live without an alcoholic of their own, eh? Well, my mom's been in that outfit longer than any of the rest of us have been sober!"

I paused and nodded to the room as another laugh rippled

through it.

"And remember I told you what the Medicine Man said to me, before we went our separate ways? That I should trust my judgement and follow my heart, eh? Well, that's what I was doing out there, you know."

My sister had moved to the west coast by then. While my uncle had been retired out there for a couple of years, before my parents moved out. And despite the nasty memories connected to my earlier time living out there, I felt no urge to drink when I got back.

"So, I wasn't having any second thoughts, and had few doubts, either, about going back to school, or changing careers, or stuff like that, you know? Because the book, and the people I knew in the program, told me it was not just ok, but right, and good, to chase happiness after getting sober."

More than any other thing, I wanted what they had.

"For me, what I wanted, more than anything, was what they all looked to have."

To get it, the book, and they themselves, made it plain. I had to stay sober and practice the steps.

"And so, when I wasn't in school, I worked on staying sober. I also got busy taking another run through the steps, you know."

Those early days back on the island were filled with optimism.

"My dad helped me a great deal in those days, and we got closer, too. I'm also happy to report we remain that way."

My dad is a rock I came to rely on in my sober life.

"And don't let anybody tell you that you've got everything there is to get out of this deal, either, my friends. Because it doesn't work like that. Nope. This program is a living thing. And it grows with you, no matter how long you've been hanging around these rooms, if you let it, you know. That's right. It grows and changes with you. All you have to do is take it along for the ride."

No matter where life has led, the living program helped me get the most out of it.

"That's what the Medicine Man's words meant to me, eh?"

After meeting the Old Man, I became more willing to look beyond the literal for meanings, too.

"So, when I went back to school, it seemed almost like taking on a kind of spiritual quest, you know?"

To me, it was more than symbolic.

"I mean, it was sort of like mentally tearing down an old me and rebuilding a new one, eh?"

Of course, I wanted the new one to be better.

"And I knew my dad, and mom, and my sister, and the Old Man, and my sponsor, too, all supported what I was doing. Not only that, but I also thought they knew how I felt. Though I didn't share that with anyone. Not right away, anyway."

For me, a white man living in Canada's snow-white world, it made no sense to be claiming positive feelings towards Indigenous culture.

"To everyone else, my going back to school was sold as a means to an end, and nothing more, you know. I kept the cultural stuff to myself."

By then into my thirties, there was plenty of fear, too, when I chose to again change careers.

"What I remember best is, despite how scared I was to be going back to school, it still seemed like the right thing to do, you know?"

The program gave me the courage I once thought booze might.

"Not only that, but getting me there took the courage I could never find in a bottle, you know? Maybe taking the steps gave it to me? I don't know. But my friends, though I'm not sure about that, what I can tell you is how grateful I am for it."

I always will be, too.

"Because going back to school turned out to be big fun. And to my surprise, I did well, too."

I remember my confidence soaring with the classroom success.

"It seemed the longer I stayed sober, the more I was learning about me, you know?"

There was plenty to learn, and I remember being surprised by much of what I found out, too.

"That's why I like telling newcomers to keep coming back, you know, because there's something new to find out here, about you, every day. And that's another part of the magic of this whole deal, eh? That it's new every day, I mean."

Just as the book says, it's a one day at a time program.

"For all of us, too, my friends. It's just one day at a time."

I paused for a sip of water and waited for the applause to end.

"Anyway, right after grad, I hustled, you know, and got my shingle hung out as a pro photographer pretty quick, too, eh? And let me tell you, I loved it then, and still do, today."

For me, it's because of the people.

"But, while I was going to school, I met someone who changed my life in ways I couldn't have imagined."

I smiled at my wife, who sat next to my dad in the front row. She nodded back, encouraging me.

"Now, in the book, you'll find a whole chapter on the perils of romance, and the power of the imperious urge, you know. And like I told you before, it's the real goods, my friends. Not only that, but I don't deny making a fool of myself trying to be a poster boy for it, more than a few times, too, eh?"

I've since made many amends because of things done in those early years of sobriety.

"But when I started college, I wasn't looking for romance. After all, at the time, losing my job for messing around with a pair of colleagues was still a recent and painful memory, too, you know. So, when I met my future wife, getting together wasn't on my mind."

When we met, my future wife was studying to be a nurse.

"Not only that, but my track record had pretty much convinced me true love wasn't, you know?"

There was a resentment growing inside me. As it often does, it wore the disguise of a cynic.

"Well, and lucky for me, I guess she had other ideas."

My wife remains a driven woman.

"So, when I hit her with the usual bachelor charm, she brushed me off. But somehow, she made it clear she liked me, too. At the same time, I mean, eh?"

School turned out to be a load for me, though, and I was often too tired for much beyond weekend program meetings until after classes ended for the year.

"Anyway, my wife is good looking, you know? And I'm persistent. Because going back to school gave me all I could handle, eh?"

Yes, it was. I still remember how, right away, hitting the books took most of my free time, too.

"But I didn't really leave her alone, or go away, either, you know? Though, between homework and weekend meetings, we only saw each other here and there, on campus."

On different course tracks, we rarely met.

"I made sure to share a word or two, though, or even just a wave, whenever I saw her at school, you know, for most of the semester after we met."

Maybe I was gun shy when it came to romance. I'm not sure. But I was helping my dad with program stuff when he needed me to in those days, as well.

"Because like I told you, I was taking another run through the steps, and working on a moral inventory when classes started, too, you know. As well, I helped my dad with his home group and service calls at night. So, it wasn't like I had a bunch of extra time or energy for chasing girls in those days, eh?"

While the imperious urge was, as ever with me, plenty strong, my want to stay sober was even more powerful.

"So, we got to know each other, at about the same time as I was getting to know who sober me was, eh? Because it's a living program, that's what my sponsor told me, and that's what my mom and dad both did. You know, they lived it."

Only getting sober and taking the steps allowed me to learn to live that way.

And just then, I thought of my sponsor and friend Blaine,

and the fearless example of program living he set in those early days when I was first getting sober.

*

"The Medicine Man later told me it was the grandfathers," I said, "who touched me, and that he was grateful to meet a man so favored by the spirits. I don't know what it was. Maybe just the feel of steam against my skin or sweat rolling down my back."

In that place with me the first time, along with the Old Man, were best friend and roomie-slash-counselor Steve, a forgotten member of the venue staff, and my younger brother Travis.

"But in my heart, then, and now, I believe my dad put a hand on my shoulder in there."

It was as real as the high mountain sunshine greeting us when we emerged from the absolute dark of that steaming sweat lodge.

"If I'm remembering it right, after it was over, the Medicine Man told me to come again, and for the rest of that summer, I did."

Until meeting him, I had only dabbled in our culture.

"I will admit I was a little shocked by what happened in there. Not only that, but I was also made curious. And I remember wanting to know more about my culture and the sweat lodge ceremony right away, too."

I recall being in a hurry to go back into the sweat lodge. Because I had more questions for the Old Man.

"And there were lots of questions, too, let me tell you, that I wanted to ask the Medicine Man."

He only nodded when I peppered him with them for the first time.

"But no matter what I asked him about, he would listen, then smile, and nod, then tell me to come back again next time."

Though he didn't say much, I kept going.

"At first, he seemed to ignore my questions."

I didn't know what to think.

"Though I kept right on going back into that sweat lodge with him."

139

I went on asking the Old Man for guidance, too.

"And boy, did I ask the Old Man a lot of questions! Because my program made it ok for me to ask them. Or even to change my mind, if I wanted to, at any time. About almost anything."

It's a simple program.

"All I have to stick to is don't drink, go to meetings, and read the book."

As with most things, it's best kept that way.

"So, when it came to my culture, it was about a personal relationship with what I knew as the higher power, not anyone else's. And that's so important I have to repeat it."

I paused a moment to survey the room in front of me, but didn't take a drink.

"It's about a personal relationship between me and my higher power."

I nodded to the room as a low rumble passed through it.

"That's right, it doesn't matter what anyone else, anywhere, is doing. Nor who they're doing it with, or how many times they do it, either. Not to me staying sober. All that matters is the relationship between me and my higher power, as I understand it."

I paused again, this time taking a drink from the water glass before speaking.

"And I'm not sure how, but the Medicine Man, and those afternoons in that sweat lodge, shook my faith in what I thought I knew."

Though I was unaware of it, what my little brother calls the doors of my imagination had been closed.

"Because by then, there might have been an unhealthy level of self-will creeping into my life. To me, maybe it looked like I had things figured out. After all, I had a good job, a nice home, a new car, plenty of girlfriends, the respect of my peers, and money in the bank."

Maybe I forgot how bad things had been for me?

"On top of that, I was sober for years by then."

Another of the many enemies of healthy sobriety is

complacency.

"So, I might have been getting a little smug in my sobriety when we all landed at that mountain resort."

Old habits were starting to plague me.

"At home, maybe there were too many girlfriends calling? Surely gambling was taking up too much of my time, if not money. And like I told you, maybe I thought I had life, and living sober, figured out."

I don't remember being too concerned by any of it.

"So, when that sweat lodge slapped me in the head out there, I must have needed it."

Maybe a part of me knew there were clouds on the horizon.

"Anyhow, my deal changed in there, and right away, too. Because from that day, I was sure there was a lot more for me to learn. Not only that, but I wanted to know more about it. No matter what I might find out."

I felt that pulling thing, towards whatever it was I found out there, strong that day.

"And though I didn't know it then, for me, the search for cultural awareness was going to change my picture of everything I thought I already knew. Not only that, but that weird feeling of being pulled onward, by who knows what, took hold of me again. So, not only what we call the real world, but that of the spirits, seemed to be talking to me out there."

Despite being more than seven years sober, meeting the Old Man proved a life-changing event for me.

"And in case there's any doubt, for me, this is a spiritual program."

Here, that goes for living, too.

"But don't get the wrong idea because there isn't anything religious about what I do here, and that's a fact. This program is about getting sober, and that's it."

After getting sober, of course, a person is free to live the life they choose.

"But there's an old saying that goes something like when the student is willing, the teacher appears. So, maybe that's what happened."

It's most likely I'll never know, for sure. And I'm ok with that.

"While I'm not sure about that, by the time we left that Rocky Mountain resort, the Medicine Man had agreed to guide me as I searched for cultural awareness. And, in time, what I found there would change my view of the world and myself."

Because it's a living program.

"And thanks to this program, which, at heart, friends, is a practical guide for living, my changing take on the world makes no difference to me not drinking, going to meetings, or reading the book."

The more I knew, the better I understood how little I had known.

"So, over the next years, I searched to my heart's content, and took only what I needed, and left the rest, from whatever beliefs made sense, and worked, for me. The Medicine Man encouraged me and put no limits on what I pursued. Same thing goes for this program. What's more, at no time did the search for either culture or knowledge threaten my staying sober. If anything, the quest made being that way even better for me."

It was what I imagined a first drink of water might be, after a long walk through a desert without any.

"At first, caution was the word. But that would change and checking out different therapy and treatment systems would also grow from what seemed a natural desire for knowledge, sparked by awareness of my roots."

More newfound confidence came along with knowledge of who I was.

"And so too did my career take off, as I opened myself up to change."

I moved to Calgary less than a year later. It was only months after Steve returned to the west coast.

"All of it, from the job that let me meet the Medicine Man, to the awareness of my culture that set me free, the many colleagues met at workshops around North America, and countless clients it was my honor to serve over the years, all of

THINGS I CAN'T CHANGE

them, my friends, were gifts I received because of getting sober."

Each day, I'm nearly overcome with gratitude for the abundance.

"So, I'm willing to do whatever it takes to stay that way, and that's a fact."

That includes calling me on my bullshit.

"Which means getting honest with myself, and thanks to this program, and many of the good people in it, I've done that well enough to stay sober for a few days now. Because, for me, no matter how long I've been sober, staying that way takes vigilance. After all, I've always been my own worst enemy, and my brain is for sure out to get me. And that, my friends, is also a fact you can take to the bank!"

I paused while a ripple of laughter moved through the room.

"Fortunately, it's a living program."

I took another short pause, this time for a sip of water.

"Because life goes on, and my living problems drove me to drinking in the first place, that's what the program taught me. So, to keep from drinking again, I need a way to deal with them, not all at once, but one day at a time. Just like it says in the book."

I nodded, more to myself than the room, before continuing. And just then, I thought of my brother Travis, and how he struggled to find and accept his own higher power during that summer in the Rockies long ago.

*

"And my big brother likes to tell people we've just met I was born on a cloudy day," I said, "and that's why my skin is so pale, compared to everyone else in the family."

I've always had a special appreciation for his joke, too. Because a thing I learned early in my life is that passing for a member of the dominant culture brings great privilege.

"But it's also true that I've enjoyed a privileged life, mainly because of my white-passing good looks."

I paused while notes of uneasy laughter emerged from here and there among the unseen crowd.

"And though plenty guilty about that, I'm also smart enough

to be grateful for the countless breaks I've been granted because of it."

When compared to other members of my family, equally talented but with darker skin, the number of chances I'm given looks outrageous.

"Lucky for me, the Medicine Man was wise enough to see I was hiding in plain sight."

I still recall the way he greeted me.

"You're the Redbone, was his greeting to me, in broken English, when I shook his hand."

I recall how the deep lines around his mouth curled, and his twinkling brown eyes danced as a smile spread across his face.

"And I replied yes, I am, uncle, thank you for knowing."

It was another big moment passing, and I was again, as usual, clueless.

"Even now, I can remember how being near the Medicine Man seemed to slow the beating of my angry young heart."

To me, he looked to have walked off the set of a Hollywood western.

"The Medicine Man was about my height, only average for the times, with dark eyes dominating a face weathered but still chiseled, despite his years. He was rail thin and wore long braids. Beneath his dark tanned skin, I could see corded muscle in the places where clothes made of leather exposed an elderly, but also fit, and supple, body covered by them."

I recall many of the kids were stunned into silence, and made fearful by his arrival.

"He was, apparently, quite pleased to meet me. So, when he invited me to join the first ceremony in the sweat lodge, right there, in front of everyone, my ego was much too big to let fear stop me. So, I agreed to be there, on the spot, too."

Though curious, by that point I had given little thought, and done less research into my Metis heritage, than I'm proud to admit.

"But maybe I was a little scared of what might wait for me in that sweat lodge, even if it turned out to be nothing."

THINGS I CAN'T CHANGE

Besides, in those times, being a half-breed wasn't celebrated in too many places. At least, none I had been to by that point in my life.

"Anyway, other than getting my brains beaten out in a boxing ring fighting under assumed names, I was also learning the trade that today earns my living then. On the side, of course, and failing at it, too, in a big way."

In getting sober, I took an extended time away from my old life. And while living in the dreamscape of those mountains, I lost the support of most people, then working on behalf of my different careers.

"Then I pulled my disappearing act."

To, as it turned out, get sober.

"Which turned out to be a good idea, because that's how I got sober."

No matter what I tell you, the words can't show the depth of my gratitude for that.

"But I told nothing to anyone about what I was doing. Neither before nor after I did it. And mostly because of that, by about six months later, there was no agent, no mentor, and no editors or publishers interested in reading what I was writing."

Which turned out to be good luck for me. Because, in those times, what I wrote was mostly garbage. Unlike the sparkling prose I've gifted you with here.

"And when the Medicine Man offered to answer questions from people taking part in the ceremonies, it seemed almost too good to be true. For me, anyway. So, over that summer, I joined as many of them as I could. And I quizzed him about all kinds of stuff that concerned me then, too."

To this day, recalling the Old Man's patience with me brings a smile to my face.

"But the answers he gave were neither clear nor precise."

At least, not to impatient me.

"They were consistent, though, and much like the message I got from this program, that was enough to keep me coming back."

Maybe it was something similar that kept me writing, despite years of rejection and failure.

"And by then, maybe what I wanted most was what my big brother, and his roomie, and many of the people that hung out with them, all had. I'm not even sure now, and I absolutely wasn't then."

Still, I searched for something more to explain their sobriety, beyond not drinking, going to meetings, and reading that damned book.

"But I didn't tell the Medicine Man anything about that."

The steps, for me, were still too simple in their beauty to be appreciated. Just then, I was living in fear of taking more of them.

"Though I doubt it would have made any difference to him if I did."

I recall growing more desperate to find and accept something as a higher power.

"Instead, I asked him for career advice, because my work has always been the crutch on which I most often lean. In those days, I did that to excuse assorted defects of character, and to avoid answering for many personal failures."

That roughly describes my habit to this day. Because in these parts, it's about progress, not perfection.

"And don't get the wrong idea, either, because my work still consumes far too much time and energy. Not only that, but just as it always has, it does so at the expense of most other things in my life."

Though neither prolific nor popular, I know how to play a hand.

"But, for me, first things come first. And so, the only thing that comes before the job is this program, and that means not drinking, in these parts. Because this thing is about progress, and not perfection, my friends."

Nowadays, despite plenty of learning, my take on getting sober has changed little.

"So, when the Medicine Man pointed to the distant highway,

that we could see from where we stood next to one another, with steam rising from our bodies in the late August sunshine after leaving the sweat lodge, it was easy enough to see where he was looking."

As I recall it today, despite something of a language barrier, the Old Man knew that too.

"Is that what brought you here?"

He asked me the question without a prompt.

"And of course, I answered yes."

He nodded, and the same open-hearted smile he flashed when we met, again creased his face before he spoke.

"Me too, he replied. Then he looked at me, and smiled, the way he did when we first met."

I remember nodding back at him, mystified.

"But I didn't know what to say. So, I made no reply. And after a pause, he spoke again."

I recall the heat of the sun drying the sweat on my naked skin and how cars on the distant highway were ants in the distance.

"Follow it, he told me."

We stood next to one another with only towels around our waists.

"Follow it where, uncle? I asked him."

The song of countless unseen birds rang from the fading remnants of the boreal forest surrounding us.

"Where it goes, nephew, he told me."

I again made no reply.

"He pointed to the highway again, then told me, follow your story where it takes you."

Only a few moments after he spoke those words, my life started making sense to me.

"And I remember how just then, when he smiled, it made him look like a long-haired but benevolent mystic. Who had just dropped in out of a nineteen-seventies movie about hippies, or something, you know?"

I paused while a moment of laughter passed through the room.

"But I was hanging on his words."

The next ones were prophetic, though I didn't know it.

"The time for telling your story will come, he told me."

In the rear-view mirror, that memory remains surreal.

"I also recall, and well, the impact of his few words. Because they were far more than audible to me. For a minute, it seemed like the wind might carry me away just then. But from that moment to this one, my life has made sense to me."

The Old Man's words resonate within me to this day.

"Because along with the end of that summer was coming a reckoning, and the only thing my pride wanted to accept at the time was a return to the boxing ring."

By then, I had not yet figured out the road went on forever, with or without me.

"So, when we all parted ways up there, my plans included little beyond clearing more wreckage of the past. Because, one day, soon, I wanted a second chance at the career booze had taken from me."

Again, I didn't share any of that with the Old Man.

"Little did I know that life had made other plans for me."

I grinned at the memory of my arrogant younger self. Lucky for me, it's a living program.

"But I knew nothing about that, when our summer in the mountains ended, and there were plenty of unknowns waiting back in the world, too, for me."

I did not again see the Old Man. For he long ago departed this mortal plane. But, along with the wisdom of those words he shared, he lives on in my heart.

TEN

"So, when I got back to Edmonton, after a phone call with my trainer, I stuck around only about long enough to pack."

For me, as with any pirate, the need to leave a safe harbor was still both urgent and real in those days.

"Before catching a lift with a sober truck driving friend and heading back east."

To say doing my thing makes me happy is an understatement.

"I was also flush with cash, thanks to the summer camps, and my old Winnipeg hotel was happy enough to hear from me. They agreed to have a room ready when I got there."

Even then, it mattered little on what I might be working.

"The morning after hitting town, along with my manager, I met with a local promoter."

As did my father, I believe a man needs something to do.

"A career restart would first mean coming back to life as someone else."

Though told few details of the plan, elder brother Blaine supported my return to Winnipeg.

"But I kept that to myself."

I remember the Old Man's words ran through my head, over and over, like the hook line of a pop song.

"At first, anyway. Because there was quite a bit of doubt about what I might have left in the tank when I first went back to the old life."

Even to me, outside of a boxing ring, much of the old fire was missing.

"Because without the nightly boozing, I was a much tamer copy of myself, and even I knew it."

Though I was far from calm.

"But there turned out to be no reason to worry. Once my hands were wrapped and I warmed up, it was easy enough for me to put on the thousand-yard stare."

I won't deny being an angry young man. Nor that I enjoyed handing out the brutality known only to professional fighting men.

"Not only that, but getting sober let me get in shape, for maybe the first time since my teens, and it showed. Right away, too."

I didn't know it then, but the heartless racket brought the worst out of me. Nowadays, I'm sure that's why I loved it, too.

"So, by the time I was a year sober, I had made it through the steps, moved back to Winnipeg, and restarted my boxing career. Not bad for a fellow who had been drunk since his early teens. That's what I told myself, anyway, as I recall."

At the time, I was unaware of the depth of my arrogance.

"On a lark, I also applied for a student loan, and soon after getting back to town, got myself accepted into university as, believe it or not, a mature student."

I recall a letter, and being surprised, but kept it to myself. Only months after I got back, classes were to begin.

"Full of myself as I still was then, I claimed not to be surprised when it happened. And my mom was sure thrilled. But I wasn't ready for school, and even before classes started, I knew that."

Outside of the boxing ring, I was once again up to many of my former habits, too, though not drinking.

"Likewise, the sober horse thief living inside me was by then running roughshod over my attempt to live sober."

I make no excuses for what went on in those days.

"Anyway, before starting school, I moved into a run-down Albert Street studio apartment above an art gallery in downtown Winnipeg. It was only about a block from my old hotel. I stayed there while going to school."

Though many amends have since been made.

"Nowadays, the word I use to describe my lifestyle back then is libertine. But in those times, most folks weren't so polite about such things. And I deserved every bit of their scorn, too. In fact, it often seemed like I was working hard to earn more of it."

In those days, friends of the family told my mom a person with any sense should be ashamed of themselves for behaving the way I did.

"And I'm sad to say, my mom was forced to deal with too many girlfriend problems made by her son."

Though I felt no shame, maybe I should have.

"The truth is, I didn't know I was riding for a fall until after it happened. Then it took me another five years to accept it."

Because life, even sober, comes with no guarantees.

"But at the time, it seemed like everything was going right."

To me, I was, at last, making up for lost time.

"In my head, ego was telling me I could do no wrong."

Besides that, I wasn't drinking.

"The hearts breaking weren't mine, and fast times are gone before you know it. That's what I thought. Or at least, it's what I kept telling myself. And though meeting rooms had now replaced night spots, for me, a lot of times, they served the same purpose."

Soon, that rep preceded me, too.

"But we don't say what goes around, comes around, for nothing."

I learned that firsthand.

"So, when a three-fight deal was offered, with a title shot on the back end and the biggest purses I'd ever seen, I wasted no time signing the contract. Only later did I figure out training for those fights would force me to drop out of school."

To me, then, it looked to be a small ask for such a big payday.

"I didn't tell my mom about that."

I recall reminding myself how nobody rides free.

"Nor did I say anything to my big brother about leaving school."

I was sure, by then, he wouldn't be happy with many of my recent choices.

"Anyway, after signing the deal, I went to work bouncing at a night club owned by friends of the man, then taking care of my career. Though reputed to be a gangster with ties to the east coast, he treated me better than most people I've known before, or since, in that business or any other."

Just the same, that life moves fast.

"And like many people I either met or knew in that callous racket, I both liked and respected the fellow."

Maybe too fast for a man trying to live sober.

"Not only that, but I also met the girl who became my first, and so far, only, ex-wife, while working there, as well."

Even writing those words makes me shake my head.

"But much like a train on a downhill track, the momentum of my life was soon beyond my control. And the only one who didn't know it was me."

After missing exams, the university sent a letter telling me I was no longer welcome to return.

"Soon after the first fight of the new deal, though, me and the ex-wife-to-be took an apartment together. And I went to meetings, too, on the regular. And lived without the nonsense, as well, for a while."

Despite the non-stop lifestyle, I recall how, even then, meetings slowed the relentless pace of my thoughts.

"So, while she made wedding plans, I trained, worked a couple of nights a week at a night club, and tried to live sober."

I had no interest in drinking, despite the fast living.

"But like I said before about life and plans, mine were sure different from what the world had in store for me."

That might be an understatement.

"Who knows? Things go the way they do, and a man eventually has to learn to deal with the world on its terms, not his. And I was about to get a crash course on what that means."

Two weeks ahead of the second fight in that contract, I was in the best shape of my life and could hardly wait to get into the ring.

"I would fly to Montreal with another middleweight from my manager's stable, my trainer, and a corner man."

The trainer told me he had never seen me look better.

"We would get to town a week early, to do local press and promo, and have access to a local gym."

The same trainer, another man held in high regard, later told me I was only scratching the surface of what might have been.

"But a week before we left, in a sparring session with one of Canada's future heavyweight champs, a bone in my right hand broke when he ducked, and I bounced it off the top of his head."

I was born with heavy hands, and wore eighteen-ounce gloves when sparring, to protect them.

"I had a cast put on the next day but cut it off before getting onto the plane bound for Montreal."

Lucky for me, the local gym was private, and I was able to hide the injury and get through medicals.

"But on fight night, when I hesitated before nailing the kid facing me with it, he landed a haymaker on the left side of my neck that ruptured a pair of discs and left a hairline fracture in a vertebra."

The only thing I remember is a shock passing through me.

"Lucky for me, the ref stopped the fight before I was hurt any worse."

Later, video of the fight showed me held up by the ropes. As one side of my body struggled with what looked to be paralysis after taking the shot. That's a movie I hope never to see again.

"I didn't know it, but that was the last time I'd step into a boxing ring as a pro fighter."

Nowadays, I believe it's one of the best things that ever happened to me.

But just then, what I thought of was my buddy Steve, and

the challenges he faced, so different from mine, after getting sober.

*

"And so, it was another couple of years after getting out of school," I said, "when things were going well with my career, and hers too, that we got together, for real, eh."

When at last we did, it was for keeps, too.

"I don't know if I made clear what a driven woman my wife is earlier, either. Because she's a girl who knows what she wants, you know, and when she makes up her mind, a thing is as good as done. She's what you call a real go-getter, eh?"

I love my wife, but see her as a force of nature.

"And I'm happy to tell you that our wedding is one of my favorite memories, too, you know."

It always will be.

"By then, I was almost ten years sober, and my life was getting about as close to a fairy tale as anything I could imagine, too, eh? In my new career, I was doing portraits and getting into freelance work and art stuff, having a great time and making good money. While my wife was finding her way as nurse at a Victoria hospital and loving it."

I was a member of a local program group and still doing regular service work.

"At my home group, I chaired a weekly meeting, sat on our local service board, had a place in a group studying the book, and stayed in touch with my sponsor by a monthly phone call, too, you know."

For me, living sober meant leading a full life. And growing wealth was coming along, because of stable living.

"Because living my program was, and is, the reason I've enjoyed such a full life, you know. And had plenty of career success, too. That's what I believe, anyway, eh? From the soles of my feet to the tip of my longest hair, too, is how my sponsor would put it."

I paused while a murmur passed through the room. For a moment, the stage lights were too warm. And my legs, under the loose trousers of my suit, shook.

"And like I told you before, my mom is the one who got my wife into that outfit for people who can't live without a sober drunk at their side, you know."

I've since been grateful to her for that as well.

"So, our marriage, well, it's been pretty much great, and right from the start, too, you know, thanks mostly to her."

I'm my wife's biggest fan.

"Because I'm also pretty sure my wife's been my biggest fan since before we got hitched, you know."

As it says in the book, their program is separate from ours. But I'm told it helps to make life make sense for people living with someone sick with this illness.

"And I sure have known a lot of happiness, my friends, and I want you to know that all of it, every drop, is thanks to you, and this living program we all share, you know. I also want you to know, every one of you, here and in every meeting room I've ever sat in, that I wouldn't trade a minute of it, not for anything, eh?"

In my story, those words are among the truest.

"Because getting sober is the greatest gift I ever got, you know? And I've been grateful for every day. From the first one to right now, thanks to you."

I nodded as applause rippled through the room.

"And that's no offense to my wife, either, eh? She knows it better than anyone, too, my friends. Because without first getting sober, I wouldn't have met her, and could never have had any of the wonderful gifts that came along with our life together."

I owe everything good in my life to getting sober.

"But just like there's a lot more to life than drinking it away, there's much more to this program than good times, too, you know."

I took a sip from the water glass. A few beads of sweat rolled through the hair on the back of my neck.

"And I'm more grateful for that than anything else, eh?"

That's a fact, and I know it well, too, now.

"Because, for years, I found out later, of course, there were signs of things to come, you know, that I didn't notice, eh. And so, by the time there was enough going on to even wonder about it, the dang thing got a pretty good head start."

Until getting it, I had never heard of the stuff. I paused a moment. And hoped the room didn't notice my legs shaking behind the dais.

"But when you're busy loving your wife, enjoying your career, and making your dreams come true, as well as staying sober, and trying to help others get that way, who's got time to worry about getting sick, anyway, eh?"

By then, many of my dreams had come true.

I looked at Linda and smiled. The concern on her face told me she knew I was hurting. And I'm claiming here it was that knowledge which then filled me with enough strength to finish telling my story.

"So, there I was, living my best life and trying to help as many others stay sober as I could, you know? And having a great time doing it, too, eh?"

For me, every day is a good one to be sober.

"Not only that, but by the time we moved into our new home, life seemed as close to perfect as it could get, in my eyes."

But things were not well.

"Now, it's important to remember that I was a healthy fellow, you know, and all my life, too, eh? So, I didn't even have a family doctor. And aside from the treatment center stay years before, hadn't had a checkup since I was a kid, back in Montreal, you know."

There was no reason to ever see a doctor, because I had enjoyed a lifetime of good health. Despite my lifestyle.

"Anyway, a couple of years later, when I started dropping the odd thing and complaining about some pain, dizziness, and being tired, it was my wife who told me to come into the hospital for a checkup."

Months passed before I agreed to see a doctor.

"But I was busy at work and took my time getting in there

to have one, you know."

I expected to be told I needed to eat better, or to get more sleep.

"But the first series of tests led to a lot more."

Even then, I wasn't too concerned. In those days, because it had yet to progress, most of the time, I was still in good shape.

"And don't forget, there's a whole bunch of tests and other stuff to get through before you even get diagnosed; you know. And all that takes time, too, eh? So, meanwhile, life goes on, and just like my folks, it turns out I'm not one for worrying too much about my health, either."

Life goes on, regardless, no matter what's up with any of us.

"So, by the time they told me I had MS, the symptoms were starting to affect me a little bit."

I paused to sip from the water glass again and looked at the cane leaned against the dais next to me. The thing has been my unwelcome, but needed, companion for the last year.

"And sadly, though it shares a progressive nature with alcoholism, there is today no known cure for the illness."

I believe, in my case, that getting sober helped to slow its progress.

"But research continues, you know, and meantime, I approach treatment like the program, with an open mind, a willing spirit, and a committed heart."

The program helps me live with my new illness, too.

"One day at a time, just like it says in the book."

And right there, I was again reminded of the tireless support received from my program sponsor and close friend Blaine. Because he, too, stayed sober. Despite facing challenges of his own when the three of us went our separate ways after leaving that mountain resort long ago.

*

"Now, don't get the wrong idea," I said, "because I'm not going to blame the culture for sparking my desire to settle down, either."

Long before meeting the Old Man, life as a bachelor was proving a poor fit for me. Despite a promiscuous lifestyle I claimed to enjoy.

"That would be a lie. And staying sober, it turns out, depends almost as much on getting honest, with myself, as it does anything else."

Here, with me, brutal honesty is the only policy that works.

"Anyhow, don't get the wrong idea, because I'm not claiming to be some kind of paragon of virtue, either. But like it says in the book, I have to practice rigorous honesty if I want to stay sober."

Nowhere does it say I have to enjoy it.

"Though I must say, in my humble opinion, that our Indigenous culture is based on something that looks a lot like what other people call a matriarchy."

Maybe that's why I'm attracted to strong women. I'm still not sure. But my mom ruled our home with an iron fist, before and after my dad was gone. And neither my dad nor our stepdad looked to mind. Though both of them were, make no mistake, macho types.

"Not only that, but even before my dad passed, and after, too, living with our stepdad, I grew up in a home mostly ruled by my mom."

Anyhow, to me, men and women are made to live with, and serve one another. I think it's plain we make women smarter than men, too, as shown by their intuition.

"Not only that, but I won't deny that growing up in a time when everybody was shacking up, could make a man who lived alone seem a little strange."

In my day, getting labeled a confirmed bachelor most often came with a nod and a wink between straight friends. With me, as with many bachelor friends of the time, only making a habit of getting shacked up once in a while kept such talk at bay.

"But all the same, when I met the Indigenous beauty who

would one day be my ex-wife, I sure wasn't thinking about getting hitched."

At the time, I was fighting a growing problem with casino gambling.

"And let me tell you, my future ex-wife was not only a bavishing ruby, I mean, ravishing beauty, but she shared my cultural beliefs, and also did social work."

For her, ours was a second wedding.

"Once again, my friends, you'll have to pardon my gangster talk."

She turned my head in a big way. It was more than physical, too. Though I won't forget her legs.

"So, after a few years of running back and forth between Calgary and St. Albert, where she lived, to spend weekends together, I found a new job and moved up north to be closer to her."

In those days, monogamy remained a struggle for me. Though I tried my best to be true to her.

"Because though I struggled with monogamy then, she was patient, at first, and after a couple of years, I got better at hiding my slips, too."

More often than I care to admit, the fever of a gambling binge ended with a one-night stand.

"Anyhow, she said yes when I asked her."

We got married in the mountains, with family and close friends invited. The Medicine Man was there, too.

"And our cultural wedding ceremony, held in the Rockies, will always be a beautiful memory."

For me, anyhow. Because I meant it to be forever. And I'm sure she felt the same way, then.

"But our marriage didn't last too long, mostly because neither of us were ready to deal with my gambling problem."

It turned out my living problems went deeper than drinking. But I didn't figure that out until it was too late to help our marriage.

"Only a couple of years later, after losing my business and

our home, I found myself divorced."

For another five years, I struggled with gambling.

"So, it was there, living alone in Edmonton, divorced, and going through bankruptcy, that I finally made it to my bottom."

Fifteen years after at last getting sober, I had once again reduced my life to shambles.

"Because it took only a few years for gambling to take away just about every material thing in the world getting sober had given me."

My self-respect went missing, too, for a while.

"And when I got there, all that was left was this program, and you people."

I remember being surprised when everyone continued welcoming me to meetings, no matter the depth or source of my troubles, without judgement. Maybe because of that, I felt neither want nor need for a drink of booze. Anyhow, I long ago accepted that as another thing I'll never know.

"Because no matter how bad things got, in those times, I still had no interest in drinking booze. Not once. Never. Through all my worst days and nights."

One morning, as I lay in bed thinking over my misery, awareness of it came to me.

"That's when I learned what people meant when they claimed to see a light at the end of a tunnel."

Things were not good just then. And I was hurting something fierce, too. But I didn't want or need a drink.

"Because all of you were still here, and still waiting for me, or so it seemed, in the same meeting rooms where I first came to get sober."

A brilliant light in a dark place, the program and its promise of freedom waited. As ever, silent, patient, and free.

"Once again, your experience, strength, and hope showed me the way out."

For me, only living this program leads to freedom.

"By reminding me that, despite my failures, if I was willing to come back, to not drink, to go to meetings, and read the book, there could be a better tomorrow."

I didn't want to drink. And had not. But the need to gamble was a fire racing through my veins.

"And if I wanted to get better, what I had to be was humble enough to admit to myself there was a problem."

Later, it proved nearly as hard for me to quit gambling as it was to give up booze. And that had nearly killed me.

"To say the least, friends, I was amazed! And thanks to this program and you, after a years-long fight, I was, eventually, able to do just that."

To be any good, a program for living must change and grow along with life.

"Because sharing my gambling struggles with you led to me getting more of the help I needed."

My program sponsor took me to the first meeting of a different group. There, I found more desperately needed help.

"And so, nowadays, I'm also a member of a program that helps sick gamblers like me get better."

I remember being stunned to find another large group of people sharing a misery I thought belonged only to me.

"So, thanks to all of you, not only have I not needed to drink in decades, but I haven't placed a bet in many years, either."

And I hope never to gamble again.

ELEVEN

"Because life comes with plenty of its own risks. And so, a couple of years after my divorce, it reminded me just how real things could get."

When it happened, I was on a working retreat at a resort in Jasper, Alberta, with a group of colleagues.

"Maybe I was getting smug about staying sober again. I don't know."

By then, I had returned to living and working in Calgary.

"I know I was making good progress rebuilding my life in those days."

Though my gambling troubles slowed my career for a while, they didn't stop it.

"And some folks tell me I'm lucky to be standing here telling you the next part of my story."

I paused, recalling the way the sun looked too high, and the air was so clean it left me breathless up there, long ago.

"But for me, I'm here because the man upstairs has a plan."

That isn't shared with me. Which makes no difference, as my job is always the same. My part is don't drink, go to meetings, and read the book.

"Not only that, but life happens at its own speed, not mine."

After these many years sober, that no longer shocks me.

"So, back to this story of mine, where we, a group of colleagues and I, are on a one-week working retreat, maybe two dozen of us."

I recall the workshops proving a success.

"And it was a good week of workshopping too, friends, filled with personal growth and fellowship."

I remember women outnumbered men by two-to-one in the group.

"But after five days of heavy emotional work, by the time the weekend rolled around, I was more than ready for a little are-and-are. And I wasn't alone, either."

When someone put out a sign-up sheet for a weekend morning hike, I let myself get talked into going along for it.

"And so, when a guy I knew at that workshop asked me to go for a Saturday morning hike with him and a few others, I agreed, in the name of personal growth, I guess."

Because I'm no fitness nut.

"I'm also pretty sure we both figured it might be a good way to get closer to any girls who might turn out for a little exercise. But when I signed up, there were only four names on the sheet."

I might have bitched to my buddy at the eight-a.m. starting time, too.

"And three of the people going were men."

I didn't like the odds.

"Not only that, but the guy who asked me to go wasn't one of them."

While we hiked that day, he slept.

"So, as I remember it now, even before we started, for me, the morning looked to be getting off to a poor start."

Our guide, at the last minute, was called away.

"And when the resort's guide had to cancel out, I figured I was off the hook. I know I was ready to head back into my cabin for some more shuteye, anyhow, and right away, too."

But the three others in the group were not so easily swayed. And I've always believed those fitness types are dangerous.

"The other hikers, though, were in a mood to sweat, I guess, and said they were going anyway, with marked trails, good maps, and compasses to show us the way."

They didn't ask me if I wanted to go. But it was plain enough they believed me included in their plan.

"So, at the appointed hour, without a guide, away we went."

In the rear-view mirror, I'm now surprised that a bunch of clueless city-types could just wander off into the wilderness that way.

"Then, I don't remember it seeming strange, four greenhorns from the city, walking off into a wilderness. It was almost like the four of us shared a need to escape what or where we were for a little while."

I'm not sure and suppose I won't ever be, either.

"But don't let anyone tell you hiking in the mountains is fun and games, either, friends, because it's not."

Between altitude and terrain, it's a serious thing.

"I remember being nearly done-in, after only a few minutes of trudging uphill on a rough trail covered in loose rock and uneven ground."

Nature doesn't care if you're in shape, either.

"It was a nice day, but heavy rains had fallen through the week up there. Because we spent the whole time indoors, we didn't know that."

On that morning, I remember the weather was perfect.

"And the girl hiking with us was a blonde-haired, blue-eyed, cutie. So, I sure wasn't going to be the first man to say uncle. No way!"

The male ego, as usual, played a big part in our shared misadventure.

"A few minutes later, when what looked like a rain-swollen creek blocked our path, and the guy leading us suggested we wade across, instead of turning back, I went along with it."

In the absence of the resort guide, our hike leader was a strapping young counselor colleague who claimed to be an outdoorsman from Red Deer. He, too, showed no fear at the sight of the rushing waters.

"So, led by a big fellow from Red Deer we barely knew, but who seemed to know what he was doing, me and the young lady followed him into that creek."

Despite the eventual result, I'm not sure if I've ever had a worse idea.

"The fourth member of our party, a slight fellow from Medicine Hat who claimed even less knowledge of the outdoors than the rest of us, hesitated."

Maybe because of that, I'm here to tell my story.

"Anyhow, Red Deer went first, and even for that big man, it was pretty clear the water was deeper than he thought it would be. It was moving, and fast, too. I could see that from where I stood on the bank. And just before I stepped into the creek, I remember wishing for something to hold on to, like a handrail, or even a rope between us."

The girl went next, with me only a few feet behind her.

"The blonde girl followed the guy from Red Deer, and I went in only a step or two after she did."

I can still remember the way my teeth chattered when that water hit me.

"And the creek looked to be only about a dozen steps across."

After two steps, it reached mid-thigh.

"The rocks under that fast-moving water were slippery, though, and I remember thinking how bad it would be to fall."

By then, it was too late for turning back. As, just before he reached the narrow creek's far side, our fearless leader slipped and fell into the rushing waters.

"But it was the big guy that fell first, and it was probably reflex that made the girl reach out to try and help him."

Within a second or two, she had fallen.

"And she followed, too, right behind him."

Despite what I know happens to heroes, and before I could stop myself, I grabbed at the collar of her jacket. I guess I was trying to save her.

"Maybe I thought I would save her? I don't know. Anyhow, I grabbed for her jacket and lost my footing. And the shock of that cold water hitting my face might have made me scream, though it could have been somebody else, too."

To this day, the power of that fast-moving mountain stream is beyond what I could ever have imagined.

"Just like that, the three of us were carried away, while the fourth member of our hiking party, waiting on the bank of the creek, later told us all he could do was watch it happen."

He told people seeing us get taken away so fast by that swollen creek scared him so badly he had to act.

"And we're lucky for that, too. Because he ran back to the lodge to get help when the three of us hit the water."

When he got to the lodge, he was in a panic. It was nearly a mile from the creek, and no easy trip. But he made it there in just a few minutes.

"After it was over, the distance that creek carried us didn't seem like much, either."

In total, we traveled less than a couple of hundred feet.

"Not only that, but the falls it carried us over didn't even take a twenty-foot drop."

At the time, I remember thinking of people getting killed while going over the falls at Niagara in heavily padded barrels.

"But when it happened, while I was bouncing over rocks, and then falling, for what seemed like forever, well, just like people tell it, parts of my life kind of passed in front of my eyes."

The worst was yet to come.

"Then the fall must have knocked the wind out of me."

I'll never know.

"Because it seemed like I blacked out for a while."

Though it lasted only a second.

"Anyhow, I remember taking a breath and getting only water, and not being able to get any air, or see any light, for what seemed like forever, to me. But it was really only for a few seconds, if that, I think."

The blonde-haired girl, who by then I knew was named Marilyn, struggled beneath the water next to me.

"I don't know how, but me and the girl were thrown together down there. And I think the warm touch of another person, fighting to survive the ice-cold nightmare that held us, might have been what made me want to keep living."

I remember screams of bitter rage filling my head.

"Then my feet touched the bottom of the fall's plunge pool, and I pushed off as hard as I could."

A moment later, I took a breath.

"A second later, when my head cleared the water, I saw I was behind the falls."

Between the rocks and the speed of the falling water, surviving the trip we made looked, at best, unlikely.

"And I'll never know why I did it, but after taking about two breaths, I dove right back into the water."

I had to get Marilyn. She was struggling to free herself in the roiled waters of the fall's plunge pool only a few feet away from me.

"A second or two later, I dragged that girl away from the falling water to a place next to me there, behind it."

Where we then clung to a natural shelf of smooth rock.

"There was a rock shelf behind the falling water. For what seemed like a long time, but was likely only a few minutes, we rested by it."

It was covered in a slick green moss. The moss made it hard to hold on to the rock.

"While clinging to that rock, I remember trying to figure out what happened instead of what to do next."

The waters in the plunge pool, though deep because of the earlier rain, were relatively calm behind the falls.

"And we didn't know it, but our fearless leader had been kicked out the front side of the waterfall to safety."

Though bruised, as with Marilyn and me, he was not badly hurt.

"Maybe half a minute later, I heard him shouting for us, and I yelled back to him we were okay, but needed help to get out of there."

I can't say for sure now, but the relief sounded mutual, back then.

"Only a few minutes later, along with rescuers brought from the resort by our fourth hiker, the big fellow from Red Deer would help get us out from behind the falls, then holding us prisoner."

Quick thinking by the hiker from Medicine Hat led to our early rescue.

"But you know how people say sharing a near death experience with someone changes how you feel about them? Well, in my case at least, it's a fact, my friends."

It can go either way, too.

"Sometimes, it tears people apart."

Near at once, I lost touch with the fellow that led our hike. Likewise, I don't remember the name of the fourth member of our party on that long ago day. Though he was, it looked to me, a hero.

"While in others, it can forge lifetime bonds."

Since that day, Marilyn and I have spent few nights apart.

"And so, I'm happy to share this with you. For me and the girl who was there, though we're not married, we have lived together, happily, since soon after almost losing our lives in those falls."

I smiled and sipped from the water glass as a smattering of applause passed through the room. Just then, memories of my brother Travis, who as far as I know, is as straight as they make them, but the most confirmed bachelor I've ever known, crossed my mind.

*

"I left the arena in an ambulance that night," I said, "and barely recall a bright-lit hallway busy with foot traffic and the chemical smells of a hospital emergency room."

The memory is not among my clearest.

"I recollect being laid out on a gurney, and what turned out to be a doctor's face staring down at me."

I remember being surprised to see the face.

"She was talking some kind of gibberish I couldn't understand."

In memory, even her face is vague.

"Later, I found out she spoke to me in French."

But everything from that time is covered in gauze. And looking back through it now is not much better than living under it was then.

"So, not only did I not know what she was saying then, but I can't remember it now."

Besides, there was little good news for her to share with me.

"And, in truth, I barely remember the next few weeks."

I can hardly recall getting home, and nothing of the flight taking me there.

"Where the ex-wife-to-be cared for me while I healed. And I'll forever be grateful to her for that, too."

Despite lingering bitterness leftover from the divorce.

"But I remember this, and real well, too."

I paused a moment. Because it's one of my favorite memories, and I enjoy sharing it.

"At no time, not right away after it happened, and not later, when I was struggling to recover, did I ever have a want, or feel a need, for a drink of booze."

The idea didn't occur to me.

"In fact, as time went on, and the outlook got bleaker, as far as my pro boxing career went, anyway, the less I thought about boozing. Even staying sober in those days stopped being a thing I was concerned about. At least, that's how it seemed to me."

There, in the middle of losing the career for which I got sober in the first place, drinking wasn't the last thing on my mind. It was no longer there!

"Anyway, to me, I guess this part counts as my early retirement story. And did I mention how pro boxing doesn't come with a pension plan?"

I paused for a sip from the water glass.

"Well, that's right, too. But the promoter covered the ambulance ride. And, lucky for me, Canada's basic health care covered my stay in the Montreal hospital."

I got out of there as soon as my head cleared. Though I needed to borrow a wheelchair to get it done.

"So, I skipped the after-party the night of the fights out there, and signed myself out of the hospital in the middle of it, leaving for the hotel in a cab, with my trainer next to me and a wheelchair folded into the trunk."

My trainer kept watch over me through the next several nights.

"For the next six or eight months, or maybe longer, a steel-reinforced plastic collar would stand in for my neck."

I can barely recall him waking me every couple of hours now.

"Which I was happy to get, by the way, instead of having a halo bolted onto my forehead."

I think of myself as among the luckiest men ever to have lived, too.

"And I spent the next couple of weeks hiding out alone in Montreal, teaching myself to walk, and learning to use my tongue again, so I could talk a little better, before flying back to Winnipeg."

I will always be grateful to the local promoter, and his team, too, for their help.

"My manager, with help from the local promoter and his people, took care of me while I stayed behind out there."

He paid for the extra weeks in the hotel for me and my trainer, and the changed airline seats, too.

"I've always been grateful to him for that. And won't ever forget the kindness spent on me there, nor the money, either."

The car, driver, meals, and meds were supplied, and paid for, by him.

"Still, when I made it back to the gateway to the west, I was pretty keen on keeping a low profile, even for me."

The press reported only that I had lost a fight in Montreal.

"Because let's face it, I've always been a secret agent."

Few knew I was hurt. None knew how badly.

"Despite having lived, for most of it, quite a public life."

Though I didn't know it, I was retired. And to this day, I've made no public statement announcing it.

"Anyway, like I told you, between my training and the ex-wife-to-be nursing me, I was back to something I could pass off as healthy in less than a year."

Few others stuck around after the wow finish to that part of my life. So, there were fewer people around to dispute my claims of good health. Which made them more convincing. At least, that's what I believed.

"Not only that, but three months later, we got married."

Though it didn't last.

"And if I had even a dollar for every time, when I thought I had things figured out, I might be a rich man by now."

At least, that's my claim.

"Because I sure believed I did, right about then."

Life, as usual, had other plans.

"But less than three years after that, we got divorced."

Since, I have lived mostly as a bachelor.

"I won't bore you with another heartbreak story about that, either. Because we all know how it goes."

Not only that, but I gave up wallowing in self-pity long ago. Though not before getting to know it real well. And that's a fact.

"Besides, I've been taking my time gabbing up here, and you haven't got all night."

Not only that, but when heartbreak doesn't come with the turf, most times I've been able to find it.

"Anyway, more than heartbreak followed the end of my boxing career and marriage. And soon enough, it would pay big dividends, too, for me."

Though, sadly, to date, it's produced little cash.

"Because by then, I had met some old timers hanging around this program who liked to say when one of life's doors closes, the next one to open will be made of gold."

Who am I, a sober drunk, to doubt their words?

"Well, once again, they turned out to be right."

Besides, who knows if I ever quit the ring unless somebody made me? Everyone knows where that road leads. I'm grateful for not traveling it.

"And don't get the wrong idea, because so far at least, it's been a life of happy obscurity for me, writing about what I do."

That racket, too, is a tale of principle, not personality.

"I've never known where the stuff comes from, either."

To me, it's something of a mystery wrapped inside an enigma.

"Though, once in a while, when it's going well, or something sells, I like to blame this program."

Because I know I couldn't be who or what I am today without it.

"Anyway, like I told you earlier, since long before getting to that mountain resort a few years before, I had been writing."

Then, as now, I had no connections in the literary world.

"Though I was having little success and getting less encouragement."

In my lifetime, I may have read more rejection letters than any other thing.

"But maybe it was trying to live like a normal person, getting married, settling down, and working a day job. Maybe that convinced me. Anyway, I doubt I'll ever know, for sure."

What I know is what happened.

"So, all I can tell you about is what happened."

That was plain enough.

"Which doesn't really seem like much, even to me."

Even then, there was nothing I can point to by way of explanation.

"Because it didn't happen for me the way it did with boozing, when I had the weird shock thing go down at the lounge door. No. Not at all."

Even today, what I'm most aware of is how it's not a sure thing. Because I don't make widgets.

"And like I told you, I'd been trying to write for years, long before I climbed into the squared circle as a teenager."

It's more of a fever that comes and goes.

"But one day, while reading the latest rejection letter from some long-forgotten magazine editor in response to a short story I'd submitted, I knew."

Though a different thing, the certainty of my knowledge is much the same.

"By then, I had already come to believe, for quite a long time, too, that I would never need to drink booze again."

It's the only thing I know, that's sure.

"I still don't know when, or how, I came to know it, but I did."

And I still do, too.

"But right there, at that moment, reading about my failings, as described by an unknown fellow scribbling somewhere far away, I knew my actual dream was not only alive, but coming true, too."

The Old Man's words then appeared, in a banner waving at the front of my mind.

"Because, just then, almost like thunder, the words of the Medicine Man, spoken to me in the mountains years before, rumbled through my mind."

On that day, I hadn't thought of him in a long while.

"First, I must follow the road before telling the story of it, exactly as he, so long ago, had told me."

In that moment, I understood the wisdom of the Old Man's words.

"Maybe I should be embarrassed to admit that it took me so many years to get what the Medicine Man was trying to tell me, but I'm not."

Instead, I'm thankful.

"Because I'm too busy being grateful for them. And him, too."

As it turns out, his words helped set me free.

"While trying to scratch out a living, one word at a time."

Which, believe it or not, is tougher than it sounds. Even if, such as I, you're better at writing them down than spitting them out.

"Because it's a living program, my friends, and I seek progress, not perfection. One day at a time."

I paused and reached for the water glass as a wave of laughter passed through the unseen crowd. And just then, I thought again of my buddy Steve, and his steadfast commitment to getting the best out of life.

*

"Now, don't get the wrong idea about it, either, you know," I said, "because living with this thing is no picnic, any way you want to look at it, eh?"

When the doctor first told me, I was terrified. On many days, I still am.

"In fact, when the doc first told me what I had, and then explained what that meant, it scared the smile right off my face, you know? And I'm not kidding, boy. I don't think I've ever been more scared, either, eh?"

I don't know if I'll ever be comfortable telling what happened next, either.

"Now, this next part is tough for me, you know."

I nodded to the room before speaking.

"Because I'm not really sure what happened in the doc's office, eh?"

To me, it was akin to déjà vu. At least, my idea of what that might be.

"All I know is, for a moment there, I wasn't, you know?"

It wasn't an out-of-body experience, either. No. What I had was an in-my-head thing. But that sure didn't make it any more fun. And nowadays, I look at it as a spiritual experience.

"You see, all of a sudden, it was like I moved back in time."

For a minute, I might have lost my grip on reality.

"So, there I was again, at the club, speaking for the first time, at a meeting. And I'm shaking, and fighting to hold back tears, you know, and desperate for help, and wanting a drink, and not wanting it, and hating myself, and the world, and so, so, sick, and trying not to puke, and almost crazy from that fear, eh? All at the same time."

In a rush, the place had changed, and instead of staring at the doctor, I was looking out at a crowded program meeting room.

"And my head is so overfilled with monsters and nightmares that it just starts exploding out of my brain through my forehead, instead of my mouth, eh? The next thing I know, it's like there's a huge rhino horn growing out of my head! Then I start just puking out this kind of verbal diarrhea, you know?"

The imaginary crowd in front of me only nodded, impassive but visibly sympathetic, as grotesque madness spilled onto them from within me.

"But I couldn't stop, you know, and the poison kept rushing out of me, and I knew the people listening must surely hate me now. Because I was showing them what a dirty bastard I really was, eh? On the inside, I mean."

That's what I believed.

"And the fear of telling them the truth about me was only outweighed by that of lying to them, or keeping my mouth shut, you know, and I couldn't stop."

The more I told them, the smaller that devil's horn sticking out of my face became.

"But the more I told them, the less it hurt me."

At that moment, it was as if someone else was guiding my thoughts.

"Though I had no idea then, or today, what I said to them."

Just as quick, I remember the memory letting go.

"Then the memory lets me go. Just like that. I was back with the doctor sitting across from me. And it looked like he was talking to me. But I had no clue what he was telling me, eh?"

For a minute, it was as though he wasn't speaking English.

"And I don't recall answering him, either."

I was bewildered.

"Because when the episode passed, I was a little out of it, eh? But I said nothing to him about it, so he probably didn't even know anything happened."

Everything took place in my head. I remember being stunned, as though I'd been in a car crash.

"Still, I wasn't in shape for talking sense for a minute there, either, you know?"

Right from those first moments, my wife Linda showed me what, for better or worse, meant.

"But my wife was with me, and she noticed something was up, eh? So, without a word, she picked me up right then. And she's been with me every step of the way since, too, you know."

For me, love is action.

"See, I wasn't facing the thing alone, not then, and not now. And that's made it a lot better. For me, anyway."

I've been on the receiving end of plenty, too.

"Though I still can't imagine how bad this thing was or is, either then or now, for her."

Nor can I save us from what is on the way.

"But I'm sure grateful to have a living program to help me deal with it. One day at a time."

To me, every day of sobriety is a blessing.

"And like I told you, it's a progressive deal, you know? So, not long after learning about it, I threw myself into fighting it off. Not only that, but I'm also blessed to have a registered nurse for a wife, and a career of my own that doesn't rely on too much hard labor."

I continue working in the career I love, too. And intend to do so for as long as I'm well enough to get the job done.

"But the truth is, when the doctor told me I was sick, and then went into detail about what it meant, like I told you, I was pretty dang scared, eh? And I mean to the core, friends."

I remember wanting to cry. And how the hospital room was bathed in sunlight, as my wife and I sat across a bare metal desk from a middle-aged white male doctor I barely knew.

"Because, to that point, I'd never thought too much about my health, let alone living with an illness other than alcoholism, you know?"

Since getting sober, my life was based on staying that way.

"I mean, it's a big enough job managing one chronic disease. How was I going to manage a pair of them?"

I was concerned, alright.

"Not only that, but when the doc told me about the physical changes that were on the way, I was pretty much knocked over there for a while."

I remember the room seeming to spin. And not wanting to cry in front of that doctor. He was then, more or less, a stranger to me.

"I was, in fact, left speechless, you know, and couldn't really think straight, for a while, either, eh?"

And right then, Linda had stepped into the conversation with the doc. While she held onto my hand.

"So, when my wife stepped in, it was quite a relief for me, you know."

I've since relied on her to watch over and guide my treatment, too. The sound of her voice, so calm despite the terror of whatever facts she's explaining, helps me accept them.

"And with her feeding him questions, the doc gave us the rundown of what to expect, in the near and long-term, too, eh?"

He told us there was hope. But at the time, I couldn't see it.

TWELVE

"I don't lie about that one, either, eh? Because it was a tough day, for sure."

One of my toughest. Either drunk or sober.

"But what I've got to tell you about, my friends, is the magic of this program. Because that's what keeps me coming back, you know, and it's why I'm here today."

Even now, the darn thing surprises me.

"And every day, it amazes me."

That's no lie, either.

"Because sitting there, listening while a stranger gave me that life sentence, not a thought of either wanting or needing a drink ever crossed my mind, eh?"

To me, that's got to be a miracle. If only a minor one.

"Not then, and not since, either, you know."

Even today, after so many years sober, it's sometimes too good to be true. And I'm grateful for it each day, too.

"Instead, when my head stopped spinning, I was already thinking about breaking the news to my mom and dad. And whether my home group was equipped for handicapped access, you know?"

I remember the way everything then slowed.

"See, I wasn't really listening to the doctor."

A calm had spread from Linda's warm but assured voice into me. In those few minutes, my wife showed me her strength.

"Because all I could hear was my wife's voice. And it told me everything I needed to know."

At once, I knew she wasn't going to leave me to face the disease alone.

"Not only that, but I knew my wife would be there with

me, you know, no matter what happened."

I still don't know how it could be possible to know such things. But I did then and do now.

"And I don't know how that's possible, either, eh, in a world built on change. But I sure do."

I smiled at Linda as she nodded to me in agreement.

"And it's all thanks to this program, and you people. Because it's your fault that I got sober, not mine. If it were up to me, I'd still be pickling inside a whiskey bottle somewhere, or maybe dead by now."

There's a certainty to the belief that after many years of living sober, comforts me. Though I'm not sure why.

"That's another thing I know, too, eh?"

Again, the only evidence I have is a faith that lives in my heart. Which, to me I mean, is real enough.

"Though I have no evidence to prove any of it is real."

It lives inside me. And I know it's there, every day, too, not once in a while.

"Because, thanks to you and this program, what I have is the experience of yesterday, the strength of today, and the hope for tomorrow."

A new illness won't take that away. Not from me. Not ever.

"And no fancy new disease is ever going to take that away from me."

I paused a moment. When the applause quieted, I went back to finishing my story.

"So, what I want to leave you with is pretty simple, you know, because I think that's the best way, eh?"

For me, keeping things simple is the toughest act to manage. I'm sure it always has been, too.

"Keep coming back."

That's it, right there.

"Keep coming back."

I repeated the words because they're worth hearing again. And again, and again, and again. Until whoever needs to hear them, does.

"If you do, it will get better."

That's a promise made in the book. So, I repeated it.

"It will get better."

But nobody has to take my words as proof. Because the book shows how it works. I'm just the still living proof it does.

"That's in the book, and the book doesn't tell lies, either."

Every day, I find more strength within its pages. In weaker moments, it lifts me up enough to want to carry on living. As the days have passed, despite an increasing number of hard ones, this program keeps me strong.

"And that's all you have to do, my friends."

Because it's a simple program.

"Just keep coming back. That's all I ever did, you know, and I'm sober over twenty years now."

They've been the best years of my life, too.

"And if you keep coming back here, or wherever your local meeting happens, things will get better for you, too, just like they did for me."

That's another promise made by the book. And kept for me, and countless others, too.

"But don't think you're taking my word for it, because you're not, eh?"

The book's promises come along with a recipe for living. And since getting to know it, I've used it every day.

"No. Because everything I've told you here today, well, you can read it in the book for yourself. I mean, aside from the personal stuff, you know, because I'm only telling you how things are for me, not for anyone else."

Only the book shows how it works. Though, by now, I look at myself as an example of what happens if you stick to the recipe.

"And that's a big deal too, eh, and I know it. Because you don't have to take my word for any of this, or anyone else's either, you know. Here, it's all about principles, not personalities, just as much as it's about progress, and not perfection."

For newcomers, getting sober is the only concern.

"So, I'm going to wrap up my story by reminding you to keep coming back. And to fake it until you make it, too, if you have to, eh? Because whatever it takes, and however it works for you, is how it works best, you know."

I paused again as applause filled the room.

"Thank you for being here, and for helping me get sober, and for keeping me that way, for the last twenty years, too, eh."

This program is, after all, a story of progress, not perfection. But just then, I thought of my old roommate Travis, and the many twists and turns of that roustabout's journey to sober living.

*

"And a selfish one, too, friends," I said, "and not only that, but I'm about as self-absorbed as it gets, and that's a fact."

Because I'm a writer and thus claim to be an observer of life's happenstance. So, keeping an eye on what's going on around me takes up most of my time. Not only that, but I recommend spending none of yours on those who make things up, too.

"And thanks to this program, I've got a personal deal with a higher power of my understanding."

The book told me it was a personal choice. So, I made one.

"And my thoughts about what that means might not agree with anyone else's idea of what a higher power is supposed to be."

For many, atheists are beneath contempt.

"But it sure works for me, and according to the book, that's what counts."

After fifteen years of booze-free living, I'm sold on the magic of this program. Because I'm living proof it works.

"So, now sober fifteen years, I'll share with you that I've also been a committed atheist most of that time. And nowadays, my higher power is science."

I paused for a sip of water. And it sounded, just then, as though everyone in the room inhaled at the same time. I grinned at them before again speaking.

"That's right, fifteen years sober."

A ripple of laughter passed through the room. I waited for it to end before talking.

"And a practicing atheist most of the way, too."

I struggled, at first, to accept the idea of the higher power.

"That's right, my favorite part of the book is the chapter addressed to agnostics, who are fence-sitters, in my eyes."

That's none of my business. Even today though, I recall how surprised reading chapter four first left me.

"But as an atheist, the book told me everything I've ever needed to know about faith, right there, in chapter four."

To me, the book makes living sober possible for an atheist. Far more than do the theories of physics upon which most of my understanding of life and the universe depend.

"If you're anything like I was, and struggling with the spiritual side of this program, I hope you don't drink, go to meetings, and read that chapter of the book. And the rest of it too, of course."

In my eyes, that book is a lifesaver.

"But get into it. And right away, too. Because when you do, what you read there is going to help you throw away the chains of fear that keep you from getting sober and living the sweet life."

It sure did for me. And there's nothing for which I've ever been more grateful.

"What I know is, for me, finding out I had been living, for my whole life, on little more than faith, in a bunch of things I didn't fully understand, set me free."

I remain so, to this day.

"Because I didn't know, until after reading that chapter of the book, that ignorance, based on contempt prior to investigation, held me a prisoner."

I still don't know how this thing works. Neither can I explain the details of the theory of relativity or the physical laws of the universe itself. Yet each of them works without my say so.

"The book showed me that the only difference between

atheist me, and spiritual you, are the objects into which each of us has invested our faith."

The investment, for me, is genuine enough to guide my living.

"Because science offers an explanation for life and death that pleases me, just as spirituality does for others."

Though neither can claim absolute proof for what we think of as reality. Because uncertainty is the answer best supported by each.

"And between them, live billions of people, each practicing more styles and types of faith than I'm even aware exists."

The book told me a personal faith was what mattered. In a higher power of my understanding.

"So, when I got that, I was able to take step three."

It doesn't matter if nobody else gets it. For me, maybe that's the biggest thing.

"And I mark that day as the end of my suffering."

The relief was subtle, but real. Though I barely noticed, everything changed.

"Or, if you like, as I do, you can call it my first day of real intellectual freedom."

There's plenty more I want to learn, too.

"And since then, staying sober is every day's number one goal around here."

Though I don't know how, the program set me free. To do whatever I wanted.

"Because for me, after reading that chapter in the book, getting sober was a matter of taking the next steps."

I didn't know it, but only then did the doors of imagination open for me. As a result, today, I accept possibilities are endless.

"Which, thanks to the help of this program, you people, my big brother, and sponsor, and of course, my sober roommate and close friend, I did. And not too long after that, I completed all twelve of them, to the best of my ability."

I have since retaken the steps a couple of times. Each trip

through them has left me with a greater respect for the power of this program.

"So, what I want to say most to each of you is thanks for sharing your experience, strength, and hope with me. Because without this program and you, I have my doubts that I'd be here today. And for that, and this beautiful life I've been so happy to lead, I'm more grateful than these words can say."

That's the news I most enjoy sharing. Though every time I do, it brings a tear to my eye. And so, I wiped it away before again speaking.

"My friends, I want to leave you with this. I hope you keep coming back. Because it works, and it gets better."

I nodded then and stepped back from the microphone. The room erupted in applause.

But I was thinking of my elder brother Blaine, to whom I owe this lengthy sober life. And just then, I hoped, again, that he knew how much and how deeply I loved and respected him. Because he always was, and ever will be, one of my few heroes.

*

"And our partnership," I said, "is another one of the best things that ever happened to me, friends."

Marilyn is the best friend I've ever had. Or ever will.

"Because, through thick and thin, since coming into my life, she's been the best partner I could imagine."

I'm sure grateful she chose to keep me in her life.

"And I've done my best to be a good one to her, too."

To the best of my ability, I have.

"But it's just life, friends, and that's no sure thing. Not for any of us, even sober. It's not always smooth sailing, either. No matter how hard we try."

The book tells me the battle with my demons takes place one day at a time. While the result is never a sure thing.

"And like I've told you, there've been plenty of ups and downs, for me, over these twenty-five years of sober living."

It's been a great life.

"I think of them as the first twenty-five, of course, and

hope to enjoy at least as many more years of sober living, too."

For me, anyhow, living sober is the greatest gift. And since not long after getting that way, I've tried to share it.

"So, today, I'm most grateful to this program, and all of you. For making a sober life filled with good times, but also touched by plenty of bad ones, possible for me."

Without this program, I'm sure I'd have none of it.

"Because without you, I'd have nothing. Of that I'm sure, friends."

I find the greatest comfort in that knowledge.

"And so, the last, and most important, thing I want to share with you tonight is more of the same experience, strength, and hope that you shared with me when I first got here."

To me, that's the stuff that makes this program.

"Because this program is simple on purpose, so fools like me can get it."

And simple, I have figured out, is often another way of saying profound.

"So, the truth of it, as I understand it, anyhow, sums to just this, friends."

I paused a moment for dramatic effect.

"Don't drink, go to meetings, and read the book."

I then stopped, while applause filled the room, and sipped from the water glass.

"When I started coming to these rooms, the people I met there told me to keep it simple, and to keep coming back."

Since then, that's what I've tried to do.

"And so, that's what I want to leave you with, too. Keep coming back! Keep it simple! Because that's all there is to this thing, friends. If it were any more complicated, I'm pretty sure I'd have screwed it up long ago!"

Making simple things hard is another symptom of my illness.

"But don't think for one minute that I'm trying to say I've got this thing figured out."

I don't have a clue how it works. Beyond don't drink, go to

meetings, and read the book.

"Because I don't really know how it works, friends."

That's true. And it doesn't matter.

"All I've ever done is what the book tells me I should."

The rest is my story.

"And not knowing exactly why that keeps me sober hasn't made one bit of difference to my staying that way, either."

I'm living proof of that.

"Because what I know now is, it works."

What's plain is that this program saved my life.

"Of course, many people, including me, don't know how a TV works, either, but nobody doubts it when they're watching their favorite show, right?"

I think of that as a show of faith.

"So, while that's a different faith than what I have in my higher power, it's also a sign that most people believe in all kinds of stuff they don't understand."

Nowadays, modern tech is the same thing as magic to most of us, anyhow.

"And it also shows that believing in things one doesn't fully grasp doesn't mean a person is out of touch with reality."

To me, that much is plain.

"Not only that, but not knowing how something works doesn't make any difference to it doing what it does, either."

In truth, life's that way, and most of the time, too.

"And I'm sorry, but for the life of me, I can't see much of a difference between any of those things, friends."

Of course, I'm no scholar, either. Nor a pop psychologist.

"Anyhow, and lucky for me, I don't have to see any. Because every day, what I can see is this program working in my life. That, and the fact I'm sober today. Now, for me, that proves how simple it is."

Though a long way from perfect, I continue making progress.

"And nowadays, I'm content to seek progress, and not perfection, friends."

It's a program for living. And getting sober is but one part of it.

"So, instead of trying to tell you how to do this thing, I'm going to say thanks to every one of you for sharing it with me."

This thing happens one day at a time.

"And I want to send a special thanks to the newcomers here tonight, too, for letting me share my story with you."

We make it work by working on its behalf.

"And please, for my sake, if not your own, keep coming back."

Though for me, the program's steadfast commitment to a principle of anonymity is what makes truthful sharing possible.

"Because this thing, and these places, were made for you."

Freedom lives in program meeting rooms around the world.

"So, please, keep coming back."

It lives in the pages of that book, too.

"Because sharing what we have with you is the only way we get to keep it."

Only giving it away makes it stay. I've heard that's called a paradox. But I don't know precisely what that means.

"And thanks most to this program, and each of you, as well, for sharing your experience, strength, and hope with me."

I stepped away from the dais and smiled as applause filled the room. Just then, I thought of something else I had wanted to tell them but didn't. Nowadays, I believe myself a newcomer to each sunrise.

END

T.F. Pruden
Thorsby, Alberta, Canada
March 6, 2023

ABOUT THE AUTHOR

T.F. Pruden is a novelist born in Canada. He spent much of his life learning to write fiction while touring the North American hinterland performing music under a stage name. After retiring from life on the road he began writing and publishing a series of literary and inter-connected fictional novels. Written in a uniquely constrained and minimalist style, they embrace the postmodern. Within them, he layers episodic and surreal elements into stories populated by Indigenous characters confronting the racism and bigotry common to life in Canada. Of mixed Indigenous heritage, Mr. Pruden is best described as a chronicler of the obscure captivated by a never-ending search for independence. 'Things I Can't Change' is his seventh novel.